Murder gets the Final Word

CHARMAIN Z. BRACKETT

DIAMOND KEY PRESS

Published October 2020

Dedicated to my beastie, Julie J. She was my bestie until an autocorrect incident forever changed our relationship. I thought Big Ben would be taller, but Hampton Court was truly amazing. I still can't believe my theater friend and I didn't go to the theater? We need to go back, and hopefully, there will be theater again when we do.

Special thanks to Pat Curry who let me feature her and Buona Caffe in my book. When I was writing a story for The Augusta Chronicle about latte art, two of her employees tried to teach me about the finer points of coffee. Despite their efforts, I am just not a coffee drinker. But if you're ever in Augusta, you have to go by there, have a cup, and have a pastry.

If you've read the series and love the books, post a cover of your favorite book on Instagram or Facebook and use the hashtag #ComeSeeAugusta. You can tag me on Instagram @ charmainbrackett.

Murder Get the Final Word is a work of fiction. Any resemblance to anyone living or dead is purely coincidental - except for Pat Curry who agreed to be in the book. All rights reserved.

Cover art by Ashlee Henry

1

My racing heart kept me from returning to a deep sleep - or any sleep for that matter. I glanced at my phone. It was almost 3. That seemed to be my favorite time to wake up from a disturbing dream. My day wouldn't officially start for another few hours, but I knew that it had already begun. It wasn't the first time I'd ever been jolted out of sleep by a haunting vision in the night, and I was sure it wouldn't be the last. This dream, however, was different. It shook me to my core. This time it hit too close to home.

I dragged myself out of the single bed in the room above my brother's garage and walked over to the small couch, praying fervently that the dream I'd woken from wouldn't be true. I knew I couldn't be alone while I tried to process it.

My hands were shaking as I held my phone. I wasn't sure who to call. I knew Trevor had a busy day ahead. I didn't need to wake him so early. I thought about my brother, but he was away on Army business. Emmie's boys had been with their dad the night before, and if she was late for work, it didn't matter. I'm her boss, after all, so Emmie was the lucky candidate.

"Grace, do you have any idea what time it is?" she asked in a groggy voice.

"Yes, Emmie. I know, and I'm so sorry to wake you up. It's just that I had a horrible dream. Horrible. Could you come over? I need my best friend. Like now."

"I'm on my way, sweetie."

I'd been seeing a counselor for a couple of months – off and on. Things had been going well. I was able to sort through a lot of fears and guilt. I could separate my own guilt from my dreams. I no longer saw ghosts of people blaming me for their deaths. On most nights, I didn't dream at all. I woke from sleep refreshed and ready to start my day. I slept through the night, which is something I hadn't done in many years.

But this was different. I knew these types of dreams. I'd had them for more than 25 years. I was only a little girl when I had the first one. Drew had said that Trevor had told him some of these dreams were my way of processing information, of linking things together in my sleep when my subconscious mind grabbed things from my consciousness and wove them together. Some dreams, however, escaped reason. I couldn't explain them away, and I'd stopped trying.

"Please, let this just be my imagination," I whispered into the early morning darkness.

I knew my words were futile. This vision in the nighttime had all the earmarks of the dreams I'd had before. The dreams that foretold the deaths of a young girl and a conniving politician. The dreams that showed me my ex-husband was in danger and needed my help. The dreams that showed a dead professor. I wanted to prevent these things from happening. I even tried to a couple of times, but I was usually just cleaning up the mess afterward. That's where the guilt had come in.

I pulled my knees into my chest. I couldn't hold back the tears. Of all people, I didn't want it to be Jimmy Hughes.

I'd always called Jimmy my best customer, and he was. He frequently bought flowers for Peggy. Usually it was to make up for something he'd done - staying out too late, losing too much money at a poker game, or spending too much money on an antique gun. Nothing that I'd consider major although I guessed it would depend on the dollar amount. But when making up with Peggy, he always wanted something extravagant – nothing simple like a dozen roses, and definitely not something Peggy considered "common," such as carnations or lilies. Jimmy said a dozen roses after a fight would've been too cliché for him, so he'd buy three or four dozen. When Peggy wanted exotic orchids, he got them; no flower was too expensive for her. The orchids weren't the only odd or specific flowers. He bought rare flowers, but he also wanted common flowers with a more difficult twist – like blue roses.

I smiled as I thought of the many times he came into my shop. He always had a smile, even when he went through some dark times. Peggy had had a serious car accident several years before. He made sure her hospital room was filled with flowers. Even after she went home, he had me deliver flowers to her to cheer her up. When he ordered them, I was concerned about how he was holding up, but he'd turn the tables on me by cracking a corny joke. He never seemed to let life get him down.

He'd sometimes call to place his orders, but over the past year, Jimmy had made a habit of coming into my shop at least once a week. He wanted to chat with Emmie, Beth, and me before placing any order. He cleaned out my inventory on more than one occasion. In more recent days, though, his visits were sporadic. I missed his smile; his "little lady" greeting; and the kiss on the cheek I often received. I missed listening to his stories, and I kicked myself for not doing more.

I tried to fill my head with the good memories rather than the dream I'd just had, but try as I might, I couldn't.

I didn't have to wait too long for Emmie to show up. In the heat of June, she was wearing a tank top, pair of shorts and sandals and had pulled her dark hair into a ponytail.

"I got here as quickly as I could," she said as I opened the door.

She didn't get too far into the room before she turned to stare at me.

"You're as white as a ghost, sweetie. What's going on?"

I swallowed and just stared at her. She reached out to touch my arm.

"Use your words, Grace," she said, trying to get me to answer her.

I shook my head "no" without saying anything else. Then, I turned around and walked back to my couch. I sat down and pulled my knees into my chest again. Emmie sat down and turned to face me.

"You dragged me over here in the middle of a wonderful dream," she said in a half irritated, half sleepy tone, as her eyes widened at me. "Did you tell me you had a dream? I was not awake when you called, but the tone of your voice scared me. Plus, you used the best friend card, and you never do that."

"Yeah. One I'd rather not talk about," I said. "Do you remember when I told you that Trevor told Drew that he thinks I process information in my dreams?"

"Yeah, I do."

"Well, I guess this could be me processing info, but I don't know. I want you here. I need you here. I just can't tell you the dream. If I don't tell you, maybe it's not real. Maybe it was just my imagination. Saying it makes it real, and it can't be real, Emmie," I choked back the tears.

Emmie reached out and touched my hand.

"You're scaring me, sweetie," she said.

"I know. It's scaring me, too, more than you know. Can we wait until Drew gets here?"

Emmie tilted her head and furrowed her brow.

"Drew? Why would Drew be coming here?"

"If my dream is right, Drew will be here. If he doesn't show up, the dream was nothing, and I'll buy us a huge container of the premium chocolate chip cookie dough for your trouble."

Emmie nodded slowly and leaned back into the couch.

"Premium ice cream. This is serious," she said and winked. "Did you call Drew, honey?"

"No, but like I said - if my dream is right, he'll show up."

"Great, now I'm even more on edge. Well, I guess we aren't going back to sleep. Do you have any tea? I need something soothing to calm my nerves."

"There could be some in there. I don't think there's much of anything in my cupboards."

Emmie got up and headed toward my tiny pantry. I guess you could call my one cabinet a pantry. I thought there were a couple of cans of tuna and a box of crackers in there. I wasn't sure about tea.

She opened the door and stood there, shaking her head.

"Grace, what do you eat?" she looked over her shoulder at me.

"Trevor feeds me most of the time," I smiled at her. "He is a great cook."

"Well, you do have a box of tea. Since you haven't lived here that long, I can safely assume it's not passed its expiration date."

She put some water on the stove. I didn't have a kettle, so she used a small pot instead. She pulled out the pitcher to make sweet tea, but she also pulled out one of my two coffee mugs. I didn't know why I had coffee mugs. I didn't drink coffee. Most of my dishes were in storage at my mom's. I kept the china I'd gotten when Drew and I got married. According to my mother, a proper Southern lady needs good china. Not sure why. I didn't use it much, but the floral pattern was pretty. Emmie fidgeted while waiting for the water to boil.

"I can't believe you got me out of bed at this ungodly hour," she said.

I didn't answer. I tried to force the dream out of my head, but it was seared on my brain. I kept seeing the image of Jimmy over and over.

"Do you have any sugar or honey?"

"Yes, Emmie, in the cannister."

After several uncomfortable minutes of waiting for the water to boil and the tea to steep, Emmie made the sweet tea, plus a cup of hot tea for herself. She brought me a tall, cold glass. I stared at it, then looked back at hers. It was odd to have hot tea, especially in the middle of June.

"What? I've been reading Victorian romances again. They drink tea all the time," she said as she sat down."

I took a sip.

"Thanks, Em. And thanks for coming over in the middle of the night."

"What are best friends for? I'm just surprised at you being all tight-lipped over this," she said as she took a sip of tea.

"I know."

I sucked in a deep breath and waited.

The silence was deafening. Emmie knew better than to try and make small talk, so she leaned back on the couch and made herself comfortable as I slowly sipped the tea. At one point, Emmie dozed off.

The minutes seemed to inch by, and then around 4:30, I heard a car. It idled in the driveway. I could picture Drew sitting in the car, pondering the time of day and wondering if he should come back after dawn. I could see him hesitating. Then I heard the car door shut. Emmie snapped into a seated position. I stood and walked to the door. I closed my eyes and grimaced, waiting for the knock. I took several deep breaths. It took longer than I expected. I could imagine Drew hesitating again. Instead of waiting for him to knock, I opened the door to see him standing there, his brow furrowed in the morning moonlight. He slowly shook his head, and the emotions I'd been holding back burst to the surface. I covered my face as I broke into tears, his presence confirming my fears. I felt his arms wrap around me as he pulled me to his chest.

"It's going to be okay, babe," he whispered into my ear.

I was sure the "babe" was a slip of the tongue. He hadn't called me that in months. He didn't say it loud enough for Emmie to hear, though. Hearing him say his pet name for me was painful. I stepped back and pushed him away without looking at his face. He didn't need to call me that. I wiped the tears away and glanced up to see an ever-curious Emmie standing with her hands on her hips and glaring at me.

"Would someone please tell me what's going on?" she asked impatiently.

I looked at her without glancing at Drew.

"Jimmy Hughes is dead," I blurted out.

Her mouth dropped, and her gaze transferred from me to Drew.

"What she said," he said, shrugging his shoulders.

"How did - ? Never mind. That's a stupid question," Emmie said as she returned to the couch and plopped down on it, grabbing a pillow and clutching it to her chest.

"Would you like some tea?" I asked Drew as I attempted to pull myself together.

In the light of my apartment, I could see him better. His expression was grim; his eyes were heavy from exhaustion. I wondered how long it had been since he'd slept. Part of me still worried about him. I wasn't sure I'd ever get past that. The gray at his temples was more pronounced than it was the last time I saw him. I could tell it had been at least a day since he'd shaved. I could always tell that.

"Grace, I need caffeine. Since I know you don't have any coffee here, I'll take the tea. It has a little caffeine, and the sugar should help, too," he said.

He sat down at my kitchen table while I grabbed a glass of ice and the tea.

"Emmie, do you want some?"

"Yes, of course. I'm going to need all the sugar and caffeine I can get, too," she said.

I knew I was going to be interrogated. I had wanted Emmie to be there to shield me from Drew, to stand as a buffer between us. I put the tea and his glass on the table. I sat down and waited for the grilling to begin. He glanced at me.

"Well, we've established that you know why I'm here," Drew broke the awkward silence.

"And I take it I was the last person or one of the last people to see him alive," I said.

He nodded at me.

"Yes, ma'am. There was a credit card receipt in his truck. It was from your shop. Looks like it was a nice order."

I smiled.

"Yes. It was gorgeous. He took it with him. He said he wanted to give it to Peggy last night."

Drew tilted his head.

"He took the flowers with him?"

"Yes, he did. Why?"

"Don't worry about that for now; just tell me what you know."

"He came to see me last night," I said as I started my story. "But I can actually do better than tell you."

I got up and walked to the counter where my phone was plugged into the charger.

"I recorded it," I said holding up the phone.

"You did what?" Drew asked.

"I recorded it," I repeated myself slowly.

He shook his head.

"Why did you do that?" he asked me.

"Because he was acting weird. I mean, Jimmy is..." I paused. I couldn't put him in the past tense. Part of me couldn't believe he was gone even though I knew he was. "Jimmy was always eccentric, but he was keeping something from me. My gut told me that I needed to pay close attention to what was going on, and I just figured I could do one better, so I recorded it. I don't have everything. I didn't start recording as soon as he came in."

Drew shook his head as he stared at me.

"Grace, are you sure you don't want to be an investigator?"

"Positive," I said.

He let out an exasperated sigh.

"Well, then, let's hear it," he said.

I sat back down and started the recording.

2

It was like any other June Monday. Beth was off, and Emmie had already left the shop. I stayed late because Trevor had a meeting to attend. Staying at the shop was easier than going to the empty garage apartment. Since June is always a month for brides, I had plenty to do. I needed to make sure that I had flowers covered for the weekend. After they left, I'd forgotten to lock the shop doors. That seemed to be a bad habit of mine. You would've thought I would've learned my lesson, but I never seemed to.

I heard the bell jingle around 6:30. The room was flooded with bright sunlight. I saw Jimmy Hughes in the store, looking around nervously.

"Hey there, sweet little lady," he said in his usual chipper tone. He gave me his standard big hug and kiss on the cheek. I noticed he was holding several file folders.

"Well, if it isn't Jimmy Hughes. I haven't seen you in a month of Sundays," I said and laughed. "It's good to see you."

"Aw, sweetheart. It hasn't been that long. Besides, you know how it is. I've been busy trying to keep my Peggy happy."

"I'm glad to hear that, but my flowers used to do the trick," I said as I put my hands on my hips.

"I know. I haven't been in here as much as I used to. I've been starting another business, and it's taken a lot of time and money away from my Peggy. I'm here to make up for it. Her 60th birthday is coming up in about a month, and I want to throw a huge party.

9

That's why I came to you. You're the closest thing to a party planner I know, and I know you can help me. It's got to be big."

He smiled, but there was something off about his smile. And his chipper façade had started to fade.

"Are you okay, Jimmy?"

"Okay? Of course, I'm okay, darlin'," he said as he glanced over his shoulder. I looked out the storefront window, but I didn't see anything. He walked over to the door. "Shouldn't this be locked? It's after closing time. We can talk about plans in your office."

I walked to the door and turned the lock. I looked outside. There wasn't anything unusual. I didn't see any cars parked nearby or people out there. I wondered what had gotten him spooked. By the time I'd turned around, he was already in my office. I followed and sat down at my desk. I pulled out a pen and paper to jot down notes and started recording with my phone.

"Peggy's birthday is at the end of July, right?"

"Yes, ma'am. July 31. She's been talking about dahlias lately."

"Dahlias are beautiful, and they come in so many different colors and varieties, and this is a great time of year for them."

"Well, she likes blue ones. Do you think you could scrounge some of those up and make them the centerpiece?"

"Purple ones are gorgeous and then there's a deep pink almost burgundy-colored one that I love."

"I know she likes purple, too. I trust you, Grace. You and Emmie know about this better than I do. She loved those exotic orchids you got for her last year."

I smiled.

"They were beautiful. Why dahlias?"

"She likes how big they can get," he said as his eyes darted around the room.

"Jimmy, are you okay?"

"Yes, sweetheart. I'm just fine. I have a meeting I have to get to soon," he said.

"Are there any other flowers you specifically want, or can I let

Emmie work her magic?" I winked at him.

He smiled.

"Yes, hibiscus. She wants hibiscus. You know I bought her one – the plant or the tree or whatever it is. She has it in a pot in her sunroom."

"Those come in lovely shades, too. I can get those pretty easily."

"She showed me pictures of this orange one with some yellow," he said. "Can you get me some of those?"

"Jimmy, when have I ever let you down?" I asked and laughed.

A pensive look came on his face.

"Never, Grace. You've never let me down," he said seriously.

His tone quickly bounced back to its lighthearted lilt.

"Peggy loves everything Emmie does, so give Emmie those flowers as a starting point, and let her go," he smiled. "You know she put Emmie's painting on the wall with all of the other local art she has. I think it's her favorite with all those rich colors."

"I love Emmie's eye for color. When I get a place of my own, she's promised to paint something for me."

He tilted his head and stared at me for a few moments before he spoke.

"Honey, where are you living these days?"

"Right now, I live over my brother's garage."

He shook his head.

"I'll never understand why Drew Ward walked out on you. That's a move he'll come to regret if he doesn't already."

I glanced away.

"Okay, so dahlias and hibiscus. Any other flowers?" I said trying to change the subject. Everyone was interested in my love life these days.

"You aren't brushing me off that fast," Jimmy stared at me.

I took a breath.

"Drew and I have been divorced since December. My

relationship with him is in the past, and I don't dwell on it."

"I still don't understand."

"Jimmy. I'm fine. Believe me, I am."

He studied my face for a moment.

"What about you and Trevor Blake?"

"He and I are just friends, Jimmy. Nothing more."

He raised an eyebrow at me.

"I've been with Peggy all my life practically. We started dating in high school. There's nothing more important in my life than her."

His words and facial expressions didn't match. There was a sadness in his voice, and I could see the pain in his eyes. What was going on with him? And why all the questions about me.

"Jimmy, are you sure you're okay?"

"Of course. I'm right as rain."

"Peggy?"

"Oh, she's doing great. She's planning a big trip this fall. We're going on a two-week cruise. Can you believe that?"

"You'd leave your shop for two weeks?"

"Sure would. Just to be with her."

He turned his attention to me.

"Grace, you've got that worried look on your face. There's nothing wrong with Peggy and me. We're doing just fine. I want you to be happy, little lady. And I've heard so many things about you and Trevor Blake. He's a fine man. I think he'll make you happy for many years. Hold onto him. Love is the most important thing when it's all said and done."

I glanced down. I knew that I couldn't try to change the conversation again, even though I wanted to.

"Believe me, Jimmy. He's just a friend," I whispered.

"No, hon, when I mention his name, your cheeks get all rosy. You have a glow about you. I can tell you love him. Does he know that? Things might speed up a little if he knew that."

"Maybe?" I didn't know what to say to Jimmy.

"See, little lady, I've done things I'm not proud of. The older

I get, the more I realize the most important thing in life is being around the people you love. I'd take back so many things if I could, so many. I've hurt Peggy so much over the years. Done so many stupid things. It's only lately that I've realized how much I've taken her for granted. I don't want you doing the same thing. Your mama and daddy are fine people, and I know they want their little girl taken care of."

"Jimmy, I'm fine. Besides, I'm a grown woman, and I can take care of myself."

"That's not what I mean, and you know it. I know you're an adult and can live on your own, but the kind of care I'm talking about, you can't do for yourself. I've heard about Trevor working at that low-cost clinic. He does that because he's a decent human being. He cares about people. And people talk. They know he cares about you. And that's what you deserve. A man with a heart of gold. Trevor Blake's heart is 24 carat pure gold."

I smiled.

"You are totally correct about Trevor. He's got a great heart, and he's a great person."

Jimmy smiled at me.

"You should tell him. He needs to know how you feel."

I shook my head at him and watched as he glanced down at his phone.

"So, you said you needed a party planner. What else did you have in mind?"

He pursed his lips.

"I see how it is. You keep changing the subject. But I'm telling you the most important thing in life is having someone to love."

"I've got friends, my parents, my brother and his family."

"No, but you need that one person who makes life worth it all." He was forceful when he said that, but at the same time, his tone conveyed sadness. I couldn't put my finger on what was going on with him.

"Thank you for being concerned about me, Jimmy. I promise

I'm fine. Let's talk about your party."

I glanced at him to see him scowling at me.

"Drew Ward should be strung up for the way he treated you," Jimmy said.

I glanced away briefly but noticed as Jimmy shuffled nervously through the folders he'd brought with him.

"Please, Jimmy. Either tell me what's wrong or let's talk about your party."

"Don't let him get away, Grace. Trevor Blake, that is. You'll regret it for the rest of your life."

"I know."

He smiled. He'd won the battle of wills. I couldn't let the conversation drag on.

"Like I said – dahlias. I know they come in a lot of colors so do mainly blue but maybe some purple. That would be good, too. And the hibiscus. What colors do they come in? Does orange go with purple?"

I laughed.

"The folks at Clemson seem to think so."

"No. We're Bulldog fans. Maybe you should stick to blue dahlias and the orange or red hibiscus."

"I can do that."

"Grace, can you help me with food? I want to have it catered, but I don't even know where to start," he said still rifling through those papers. Several of them slipped to the floor. He stooped over to pick them up.

"Trevor would make a great caterer, but I can't convince him to follow his heart when it comes to food."

"I've heard he's a great cook."

"He's more than a cook. He's amazing. Since he's not an option, I think I can find a couple of people for you. If you want cake, Mama would probably make one."

"Lottie's cakes. Oh yes, we need one of those."

Jimmy glanced at his phone again.

14

"Are you sure everything's all right, Jimmy?"

"Are you sure Trevor's just a friend?"

He locked eyes with me, and a chill went down my spine. I knew something was off, and he knew that I knew. And he just confirmed it. He shook his head. He wasn't telling me what it was, and there was no forcing him into it. We were at a deadlock. He wasn't budging as he continued with his party list.

"Flowers, food. I have a venue. I think I need some entertainment, maybe a band. I don't care what it costs. I know you will treat me fairly. You always have, even though I know running this shop has been hard for you over the years. I appreciate your integrity. You could've taken me for a ride many times, but you never did."

With that, he stood up and headed for the door. I followed him to unlock the door. He paused and looked at me before giving me a weak smile and kissing my forehead.

"Don't worry about me, little lady," he whispered and then he walked out.

There was a finality in his words that I didn't understand at the time.

3

I didn't watch Drew's expressions as he listened to the recording. It was awkward for me knowing that Jimmy and I had spent a great deal of the conversation talking about Trevor and Drew.

I cleared my throat as the recording ended.

"So, there you have our last meeting."

I slowly glanced up at Drew. He stared at my phone on the table without looking at me.

"What did you do when he left?" he asked as he raised his eyes to meet mine.

"I locked up the shop and went to see my parents. You know they've been friends with Jimmy and Peggy for years."

"Did you record that conversation, too?" Drew was snarky. Jimmy's remarks about him, Trevor, and me seemed to have gotten under his skin. Plus, I doubted he was happy when I pushed him away.

"No, I didn't stay too long. They were having dinner with some friends from church. I popped in and said hello, but I asked Mama to come out on the porch so I could talk with her. I told her about Jimmy, and she said she'd call Peggy. She said she didn't know of anything that would cause him to be upset. That was the last I'd heard of it. But I did notice she seemed uncomfortable talking about them."

Drew tilted his head and raised an eyebrow at that, but he

didn't say anything. We both knew it was odd.

"Can you tell me anything about what happened, Drew?"

He slowly shook his head.

"Why don't you tell me about your dream first, Grace?"

"In my dream, I saw him leave here with the flowers. I saw him go into his office. He sat down, and I saw a couple of tears in his eyes. The next thing I remember was seeing him like he was resting his head on the desk, but I knew he wasn't resting because I could see blood," I paused as I glanced at Drew. "And a lot of it. When I woke up, I felt like he'd been shot."

Drew's mouth dropped.

"Anything else?" he asked.

"No. I can't think of anything."

"What did he do with the flowers? Did he have the file folders with him? The ones you said he brought into your shop."

I thought about it.

"I don't think they were in my dream. The flowers and the folders were gone."

He stared at me without saying anything for a few moments. He blinked a couple of times and shook his head with his brow furrowed.

"Dr. Blake may be right about some things, but you weren't at the scene, were you? You didn't follow him to his shop and peer in the window, did you?"

"No."

"You just described my crime scene. How did you do that?"

"I don't know. Overactive imagination?" I hung my head and started to cry again. I didn't want to describe his crime scene. I didn't want Jimmy Hughes to be dead. I wanted to be wrong.

"Grace, do you know who did it?" he asked. "That would really be helpful."

"No. I just know that Jimmy acted scared of someone. He wasn't acting right."

Drew didn't answer right away. He wanted to ask me

something. I could tell. He always got this look on his face when he needed to ask me something and he wasn't sure how I'd respond.

"Grace, I have no right to even ask this, but I need your help."

I could see Emmie out of the corner of my eye. She was giving me her look – the one that warned me not to do something. I usually ignored that look. Sometimes, I lived to regret that decision.

"Actually, Grace," Drew continued. "Jimmy needs your help. You'll be places where you can hear conversations. You'll probably go to the Hughes' residence and to the funeral home and to the funeral. People talk in whispers in those places."

"That they do."

"And they say things there that sometimes slip their minds when they talk to the police."

"I suppose that's true.'

"Grace, you know it's true," he paused. "Look, I don't want you to track anyone. I want you and Emmie to do what you do well – eavesdrop. Be a fly on the wall. Just listen. Don't follow anyone. Don't go after a killer yourself. Don't be an investigator. And don't do any extra research on the Internet. Just listen and let me know if you hear anything," he asked.

Now it was my turn to ponder his words. I hesitated as I stared blankly at him.

"Please," he whispered. "But not for me. For Jimmy. Help me bring justice to Jimmy's killer."

I nodded.

"For Jimmy," I said.

"Thank you," he said. "And thanks for the tea."

I followed him as he walked to the door. He paused before opening it as though he wanted to say something. Instead, he opened it and walked down the stairs without saying another word.

I closed the door. I knew my eagle-eyed friend was staring me down. I could feel her eyes burning holes in my back as I stood there. I took a breath before turning around.

"And what else just happened there?"

I turned around to see her with her arms crossed against her chest. I shrugged my shoulders and tried to play innocent.

"What did he say to you?"

"What are you talking about, Emmie?"

"Oh, stop it. You know exactly what I'm talking about. I saw you push him away. I thought he might fall over."

I put my hands on my hips.

"He called me 'babe.'"

"Ah" was all she said.

"He called me 'babe,' and everything that happened between us came rushing to the surface. Maybe he didn't mean to say it. Maybe it was just a slip of the tongue, but it hurt."

"I know it did. It still hurts when I see my ex with his wife and my kids."

She put her arms around me and hugged me. When she let me go, she still looked agitated with me.

"But you're still going to help him, Grace? Why?"

"Not him, Jimmy."

"Tell yourself that if you want to, but you know you're helping Drew."

"No, that's where you're wrong. I'm going to be nosy and find out what happened to Jimmy. And maybe I'll tell Drew or maybe I'll just solve this case all by myself."

Emmie stared at me.

"You're going to get yourself in trouble one day."

"What more trouble could I possibly get into, Emmie? I've been kidnapped twice, threatened with a gun, seen someone killed before my very eyes. I don't really think there's much more I can do. I suppose I could get arrested, but what Drew Ward doesn't know won't hurt him – or me."

She put her hands on her hips.

"Fine. Just fine. You keep telling yourself that. You're the only one in this room who believes it."

"I don't know what you're so upset about. I didn't ask you to help me. Besides. We'll be delivering flowers, and just like Drew said you and I will be at the right place at the right time. It's not like I'm going after information. I'll pick up anything that falls in my lap."

She continued to glare, so I smiled sweetly.

"You know you want to help me, Emmie. Admit it. You are dying to help me and Drew. You miss the FBI no matter what you say. Even if it was only a temporary job."

She tried hard not to smile at me, but she finally gave in.

"I hate it when you're right. I do need a little excitement in my life. My life of dateless Fridays and uninspired canvases is getting old."

I hugged her.

"Look, I believe a nice guy will come along for you. We both need to just stay away from cops, and we should be fine."

"No lie. I will never date a cop again," she said and laughed. "Forgive me if I'm late for work. Someone dragged me out of bed at an ungodly hour."

"Five minutes late and nothing more," I pretended to be angry when I said that, but we both laughed.

"I need coffee, Grace. I'll see you soon," she said as she left.

4

It was quiet when I got to the shop. Beth was off; Jazzy had class and then went to her job at the physician's practice that Beth's husband and Trevor's brother were part of. It would be just Emmie and me whenever Emmie decided to come in.

I logged on my computer and checked the newspaper's website, searching for anything I could find about a murder. There were no stories there or on the TV stations' websites either. Maybe they hadn't released any details.

About 9:15, the phone rang.

"Grace's Gifts, this is Grace. How may I help you?"

"Hello. I'd like to send some flowers," the caller began. It was a man.

"Then, you've called the right place."

"Do you have any dahlias in stock?"

Dahlias. A shiver ran down my spine. Jimmy had asked for them last night. The answer to that was "no," but my mother had dahlias in her greenhouse that Daddy had built for her as a Christmas present. She'd filled it with all sorts of beautiful flowers. They had been blooming on my last visit, and I was sure I could steal some. She had them in her yard, too, but those wouldn't be blooming until later in the summer.

"I have access to some, yes," I didn't want to lie to a customer.

"Could you make an arrangement with some? I'd like a few

roses and peonies as well," the caller said.

"Of course. I can have them delivered after lunch."

"Great. They are going to Peggy Hughes in North Augusta. I have her address."

I almost dropped the phone as my heart stopped. I felt a chill, and it wasn't from my air conditioner which was at full blast on this hot and muggy June morning. This wasn't a sympathy bouquet, and it wasn't anything appropriate for a funeral. He continued to give me her address, and on the card, he only wanted his first name "Steve."

When he gave me his credit card info, I got his full name – Steven J. Mathis. The name didn't ring any bells with me. As I was staring at the computer screen and trying to figure out who Steven Mathis was, Emmie dragged herself in the door.

"I don't think there's enough caffeine in all of Augusta to help me this morning," she said as she set her large, steaming cup of coffee on the workstation. "Aren't you tired, Grace?"

"Always, but adrenaline has kicked in," I said absently. "Emmie, have you ever heard the name 'Steve Mathis?'"

She wrinkled her nose as she thought.

"No, why?"

"Because he just ordered an arrangement with dahlias for Peggy Hughes."

"Dahlias for Peggy Hughes," she repeated slowly.

"Yes, and the card should only have his first name on it."

"That is super strange. Have you heard anything about Jimmy's death on the radio or anywhere else?"

"No, I haven't. Maybe this Steve Mathis doesn't know Jimmy's dead because this certainly isn't for a funeral. And it's not something I'd sent to a loved one as a sympathy arrangement. It's too romantic for that."

She tilted her head.

"Didn't Jimmy want dahlias?"

"Yes."

"Grace, we don't have any dahlias."

"We don't, but Lottie does," I said and grinned at her.

"Your mom would hate it if she knew you called her by her first name."

"And who's going to be the one to tell her?"

Emmie threw up her hands.

"Not me."

"That's what I thought. I need you to hold down the fort while I go get those dahlias out of her greenhouse. He wants peonies and roses, too. I think I'll have to snip some peonies as well. I have some coming in for this weekend's weddings, but I think we went through our stock with last weekend's weddings."

"You got it, boss."

I went into my office to grab my purse, and Emmie followed.

"Grace, do you think your mom knows about Jimmy yet?"

"I have no idea. I haven't talked to her yet this morning, but I'm not going to let her know about my early morning visit from Drew."

"Good plan."

I pondered texting Drew before I left for my mother's, but I wanted to get more information. The less contact I had with him the better for my mental health. Besides, I wanted to ask my mother about Steve Mathis. Maybe she was familiar with that name and person.

Daddy was in the living room reading a book when I walked in. I gave him a kiss on the cheek.

"Good morning, sweetheart."

"Good morning. Is Mama here?"

"On a gorgeous June morning, where do you think she is?" he asked and laughed.

"Garden?"

"Absolutely."

From his demeanor, I could tell he knew nothing about Jimmy's death, but before I could head to the back yard, my dad reached out for my hand.

"You okay, darling?" he asked.

I bit my lip. I couldn't hide anything from him.

"No, but I'll be okay," I said, trying not to give anything away.

"You don't want to talk about it."

I shook my head "no."

"Maybe later. I need to steal some flowers from Mama's greenhouse."

He laughed.

"I should've built that thing years ago," he said.

"Probably. I need some dahlias. I don't have any of those right now. And maybe some peonies."

"She's got some beautiful dahlias out there."

I winked at him.

"I know. That's why I'm here."

"I guess I should build you one, too," he said.

"Maybe one day. I don't think Zack wants one of those in his yard."

"How are things with you and Trevor?"

I smiled without saying anything.

"I'm going to see about those dahlias now," I said as I headed outside to find my mother.

"You know Trevor comes and talks to us," he said as I was leaving the room.

I stopped in my tracks, returning to the living room to smile at him.

"I'm glad. He's a good man," I said.

"Your mother and I really like him. We always have," he said.

"I know. I'm glad. Now, I'm going to get flowers."

I walked out of the kitchen door into her yard, which was teeming with blooming flowers and other vegetation. She'd done a lot of work in her backyard in the last several months and had transformed it into an idyllic sanctuary. She had her yard divided into her beautiful sitting area with a swing underneath a gorgeous rose arbor. Stone pathways cut through the lush Bermuda grass lawn.

In the corner of the yard was her greenhouse, and she had another section for her vegetables. One of my favorite things was her water feature, a small pond surrounded by beautiful stones and a waterfall. She had several koi in the pond.

She was on her knees pulling weeds from her vegetable garden when I saw her. Wearing a floppy hat and her gardening gloves, she was intent on her task and didn't hear me as I approached her.

"Mama," I said, startling her.

"Grace," she said as she stood up. Her expression changed from joy to concern. "Did you sleep last night?"

"Emmie and I had a late one, or an early one, or something like that."

I searched her face, but there was not a hint that she knew about what had happened to Jimmy. I was glad she just thought I'd had a late night. That's all she needed to know.

"You two. I guess it's good to have someone to stay young with."

"I don't know what I'd do without Emmie."

"So, what brings you here so early?"

"Dahlias and some peonies. I ran out of peonies after this past weekend's weddings, and I won't be getting anymore until tomorrow."

I smiled as I held out a vase for her to put them in.

She put her hands on her hips and laughed.

"I'm going to have to up my rate," she said.

I laughed, too. She didn't charge me, and she'd never let me give her any money, even if I tried.

"Well, I do have some pretty ones," she continued." Let's take a look. Oh, and before you leave, I picked some tomatoes this morning. They are in the kitchen on the windowsill. They have been so tasty this year. I added extra plant food to the soil."

"I can't wait to have a tomato sandwich."

"Don't tell anyone, but I had one for breakfast," she laughed.

"I'm not surprised."

I followed her into the small greenhouse.

"I know I don't have to tell you this, but a lot of dahlias peak in September and October around here. Good thing I have this greenhouse. I wished I'd done this sooner. I've always loved dahlias, and in the climate-controlled environment, I can pace these to have them throughout the summer. Got a big order?" she asked with a smile.

"No."

She didn't buy my clipped answer.

"Anyone I know?"

I glanced around.

"Peggy Hughes."

She smiled.

"Jimmy's in the doghouse again? I wonder what he did this time," she said and laughed. "I guess you were worried for nothing."

I glanced down at the flowers in the vase and bit my lip as hard as I could. I didn't need to fall apart, but the reality of Jimmy's death hadn't completely hit me yet.

"No, they aren't from him."

"Oh," she said with a curious look.

"A man named Steve Mathis called and ordered them."

Her face blanched, and she set her jaw. The last time I saw that look on my mother's face was when I'd told her Drew had left me. She was angry, and that was a mild way of describing it.

"Steve Mathis?" she asked slowly, but I could hear some venom in her voice.

"Yes, the name didn't ring any bells with me, Mama."

She glanced around without saying a word, then she completely changed the subject.

"Do you want the dark pink or purple? How big? I have some average size. The dinner plate ones aren't ready yet."

"Do you have blue?"

"Those aren't ready yet."

"Do you know Steve Mathis?"

"I don't gossip, Grace, and you know it," she snapped at me.

I was shocked because my mother never snapped at me. She snatched the vase from my hands, shoved the blooms in it, and pushed the vase back into my hands without saying a word. Then, she walked out of the greenhouse and went back to her weeds.

I wasn't sure how to respond to that. I wanted to ask her if she'd talked to Peggy, but that was the end of that conversation. I headed back into the house. My father was still sitting in the living room. He'd put his book away and sat changing channels with the remote.

"You get what you needed?" he asked.

"Sort of."

He turned and gave me a puzzled look.

"Who's Steve Mathis?"

He shook his head and smiled.

"Well, if things had been different, he could've been your dad, but he broke up with your
mom to date Peggy Hughes. He was never one to stay in a relationship long. He left her for someone else. Last time I heard that name, I think he was on his fifth wife. After wife 2, they started getting younger and younger. Why?"

"He's sending flowers to Peggy Hughes."

"I may need to get you to make a bouquet up for me," he said and laughed.

It bothered me that I was the only one who knew Jimmy was dead, but I knew I couldn't be the one to bring the bad news. I had to leave before I broke down and that wouldn't be much longer.

"Daddy, when was the last time you talked to Jimmy or Peggy?"

"I think your mother called Peggy last night after you came by, but she didn't get her on the phone," he said and tilted his head at me. "Is everything okay?"

"It's like I told Mama on the phone. Jimmy just didn't seem right last night when I saw him. There was something off about him. It scared me."

"I'm sure everything is just fine."

I glanced at the floor. Everything wasn't fine. I needed to get out of their house quickly.

"I'm going back to my shop."

I gave him a quick hug before heading out the door.

I knew I needed to be the one to deliver Steve Mathis' flowers to Peggy. If nothing else, I wanted to find the truth of what happened to him. Call it being nosey; call it helping Drew; call it whatever you wanted, but I knew I needed more information. I wasn't satisfied with just reading about it on the newspaper's website. I thought about calling Drew, but I decided to wait until I found out more.

5

I had hoped that Emmie didn't hear my car pull up. I sat there for a few minutes just to cry. I didn't want to fall apart when I took the flowers to Peggy, so I decided to cry as much as I could and maybe I'd be okay when I saw her. I knew that was a lie, too, but I needed to do something to keep myself going. I stared at the rich, vibrant colors of the dahlias. They were gorgeous.

Emmie was waiting for me when I got in.

"I see she had just what you were looking for."

"Yes. Aren't they gorgeous? These light pink peonies will go really well with them."

"They are. I'd love some of those for my house. Do you want me to put something together?"

"Actually, I think I'd like to do this one myself."

Emmie smiled at me.

"It's good to see you doing more arrangements. You're starting to look like my best friend again," she said.

"I was starting to feel like your best friend again until today and Jimmy's death. I think I'd forgotten who your best friend was for a long time. My therapist told me to get in touch with things that have always made me happy. Arranging flowers has always done that. Oh, and you should see Miss Harper's rose garden. Trevor has gotten everything I asked for to bring it back to its former glory. I've spent a lot of time giving those bushes some much-needed TLC."

"I can tell by the amount of sun you've been getting, sweetie."

"I wear sunscreen. Trust me, the oncologist in Trevor makes me lather up SPF-50 every time I go outside. I also wear a wide-brimmed hat."

"He cares about you," she said and winked.

That meant she wanted me to say something else, but it wasn't happening.

"Have you seen anything online about Jimmy's death yet? Have the newspaper or TV stations posted anything yet?"

"Grace and changing the subject. You are such a pro at that, sweetie. And to answer your question is 'no' for the umpteenth time."

I grinned at her.

"Fine. Be that way," Emmie continued. "No one has called about funeral arrangements yet."

"Well, there will be an autopsy, which will delay things. And Peggy probably hasn't even contacted a funeral home yet. She's probably still in shock. I know I am."

"Honey, we all are. Did you tell your parents?"

I scowled at her.

"Are you crazy? Absolutely not. They'd want to know where I got the information, and I didn't really want to tell them that Drew was inside my apartment at 4:30 this morning. They get sensitive when it comes to Drew. They don't like me talking to him."

"Can you blame them? He crushed their little girl's heart."

"I'm fine. Why doesn't anyone listen to me?"

I had pulled out a base and began arranging the flowers in the floral foam. They were beautiful. I didn't use dahlias often, but now that I had a supplier, I thought I could get used to them.

I loved learning the meanings behind flowers, but I knew that not everyone did. Peggy Hughes did, though. As I thought about Steve Mathis, I thought it was interesting that Jimmy had wanted blue dahlias. With most flowers, the meanings changed depending on the color. Pink and purple dahlias symbolized kindness and grace and the blue ones meant fresh starts and big changes. Recalling Jimmy's cryptic comments, I wondered if he thought there was a fresh start or big change coming Peggy's way. And then there were the hibiscus symbolizing the fleetingness of beauty. Of course, his death changed a lot of things for her, but he had no idea he was going to die. He was planning a big birthday celebration.

I cried as I put the flowers in the foam. The night before, I'd made a beautiful arrangement with red roses for Peggy from her husband, who kept telling me that he had loved her so much. I felt like a traitor to him making this arrangement for a former beau to give to her.

"No, really, Grace. Are you okay?" I heard Emmie ask.

"Fine as I will be. I can't believe he's gone. I saw him last night. He was right here in my office, and I made flowers for him to give to Peggy. I wonder what happened to them?"

"I don't know. You're right, though. All of this is hard to take in."

"Why did I agree to make this?"

"You didn't know who it was for when you said 'yes' would be my guess."

"What am I going to say to her?"

"I'm sure you'll think of something."

"Drew told me that she knows I was one of the last people to see him alive. I'm a little nervous about that."

"Do you want me to take it instead, Grace?"

"No, I think I need to handle this one."

"Are you planning on spying for Drew?" she stared at me. I sighed.

"Didn't we already agree that if I was helping Drew it was to find Jimmy's killer and nothing else?"

"Liar," she said and laughed.

"Well, it's not because I want to see Drew. I don't. Going to a therapist has helped me weed through my emotions. I'm starting to see things in a better light now. Besides, if I spy, it's for my own curiosity."

"I'm glad to hear it," she paused and stared at the arrangement. "That's really pretty, Grace. I love the dahlias, too. They are striking flowers anyway. I'm glad you have a supplier. Oh, the things I could do with them."

I glanced up to see her broad smile.

"I hope she keeps growing them. She wasn't happy with me when I asked about Steve Mathis."

"Hmm. I guess you dredged up some bad blood."

"Sounds like it," I looked at the arrangement to see if I needed to add anything else. Emmie was right; dahlias were striking, and I was proud of how the arrangement had turned out. "Okay. Well, I guess I need to be on my way. Wish me luck and say a prayer, will you?"

"You'll be fine, Grace."

When I arrived at the Hughes' home, there were no cars outside. I took a deep breath as I got out of the van and unloaded the flowers. I hesitated before knocking on the door. Jimmy and Peggy's daughter, Becca, answered. Becca was a couple of years older than me. She was thin but muscular. She had a mossy brown, bobbed haircut. She glanced at the flowers and then back at me.

"These are for your mom. Someone called them in this morning."

"Who is it, Becca?" I could hear Peggy calling out.

"It's Grace Ward, Mom," she yelled.

There was silence for a few moments; then I heard the sound of footsteps across the hardwood floors. I looked past Becca to see Peggy. If I had seen her on the street, I wouldn't have recognized her. She had on no makeup, and her eyes were puffy from crying. Her hair hadn't been combed, and she was wearing sweatpants, an oversized T-shirt, and a bathrobe. She carried a box of tissues.

She walked over to me and glanced at the flowers. Her eyes widened.

"I don't understand. Who sent me dahlias?" she asked.

"Someone called them in for you this morning. There's a

card."

She took them from me and placed them on the kitchen island. She pulled out the card, then covered her face with her hands and cried.

I wasn't sure what to do. I felt awkward standing there. Becca put her arms around Peggy and held her as she sobbed. I started to leave when I heard Peggy tell me to stay.

"Grace, please don't go yet. I need to talk to you," she said as she turned to look at me. "I was going to call you. You know, don't you? It hasn't been released yet, but you know."

I simply nodded "yes" as I stood in the doorway until she gave me a sign to move. My job caused me to be around grieving people on a regular basis, but after all this time, I still was never sure what to say to them. I usually didn't say much. If people wanted to talk, they would. Sometimes, they just wanted someone to listen and to care.

After a long pause, Peggy lumbered across the floor. She headed past all her beautiful artwork, including one of Emmie's paintings, to the sunroom overlooking the Savannah River. It was my favorite room in her house. As I followed her, I noticed the beautiful arrangement Jimmy had purchased the night before. It was in the center of her massive dining room table. It looked so small there. I wondered what had happened. Had he brought it home to her, then headed to his office? She sat down, but her eyes were fixed on the wall of windows. I sat down on the leather couch and waited for her to speak. I tried not to stare at her, so I allowed my gaze to wander. I spotted the hibiscus plant near the windows.

"Your mother called me last night. She said you were worried about Jimmy."

"Yes, he came into my shop. He told me he wanted to plan a surprise party for your birthday," I paused as she started to sob again. I glanced at Becca. She didn't return my glance. She seemed angry as she stared her mother. I wasn't sure why I thought that. She wasn't crying. She had a blank expression except for her tightened jaw. I've always heard about the stages of grief. My therapist talked about it when discussing the miscarriages and the death of my marriage. I'd gone through most of them. I could see the disbelief in Becca, too. I'd known Becca since we were kids. Despite the fact that our parents were friends, we weren't exactly what you'd call friends. She was a couple of years older than me. We didn't go to the same school, and her hobbies were all sports related.

"He wanted it to be a huge event. He wanted me to do the flowers and to find a caterer. He wanted it to be a splashy soiree. And he kept telling me how much he loved you," I continued even though I knew it would make her cry more. He wanted her to know that, so I wanted her to know that. "He said it so many times."

I waited for her to say something. It was awkward. I didn't know what else to do.

"You know you were probably one of the last people to see him ... to see him ... alive," she choked out the words through her tears. She pulled several tissues out of the box and patted her face.

"That's what Drew told me."

She gave me a faint smile.

"When I came home last night, that beautiful arrangement was on the dining room table. I knew he'd been at your shop. It didn't look like Emmie though. I figured it had to have been you."

I nodded.

"He watched me make it and left with it."

"It sounds like you spent quite a bit of time with him last night," her voice faltered.

"He was there about an hour, I guess."

"What else did he say?" she asked.

I hesitated.

"He seemed afraid of something, but he wouldn't tell me what. He seemed off. He kept saying nothing was wrong. That's the reason I went to see my mother."

She paused and looked at the floor.

"I got Lottie's message, but I didn't call her back. I went out to dinner last night with an old friend."

Steve Mathis, I wondered. I didn't say anything.

"I thought about calling her, especially when he didn't come home," she said. "I waited up, but the only person who came was the deputy who told me the news."

She gazed off into the distance for a few moments. She tried to pull herself together and then she started talking again.

"You're right," she said looking at me. "Jimmy had been distracted lately. There was something at the shop that was on his mind that he wouldn't tell me about. I didn't know what was bothering him."

"He didn't really open up to me. Not that I really expected him to."

"And I don't think he was too happy with me despite what he said to you. I was looking into a new business deal. That's what my meeting was about. I had an investor meeting."

"He did say something to me about new businesses."

"Well, he was thinking about doing something different, too. He'd thrown around all kinds of ideas – some crazy; some reasonable. He'd always wanted to do something with real estate. He even mentioned selling his shop. But I could never see him selling that place. He loved it," she said.

"He loved that place more than he ever loved us," growled Becca. "Why was he always there so late at night?"

"Now Becca, you're being ridiculous," Peggy scolded her daughter.

"No, I'm not, and you know it. That business was worse than him having a girlfriend."

"I'm not discussing this with you now," Peggy replied sharply.

I glanced at the floor during their uncomfortable interlude.

"Do you have any idea about funeral arrangements?" I asked, slipping into my role of conversation changer.

Peggy turned her eyes back to me.

"Not yet. I'm sure it will be hitting the news soon enough. I don't know why it hasn't yet. I'm waiting for my phone to start ringing off the hook."

She smiled faintly as she tried to lift the mood, but we all knew that wasn't happening.

"Peggy, if there's anything I can do, please let me know."

Those words sounded so hollow.

"I'm sure Lottie will bring me some of her famous pound cake. That seems to be the answer to a lot of the world's ills."

"She'd like to think so," I said with a smile. "I need to get back to the shop."

"Of course," she said. "I'm sure I'll be seeing a lot of you or at least a lot of your and Emmie's handiwork over the next several days."

I stood to leave.

"Grace, did he say anything else?"

"No, Peggy, he just wanted you to know how much he loved you. He kept saying it over and over."

That statement brought a fresh round of tears.

"Thank you for that," her voice was hoarse. "We loved each other in our own ways, I suppose. It wasn't easy, but we tried to make it work."

Peggy stood up and walked over to the windows to gaze outside. I took that as a good signal to leave.

6

I decided I wasn't going to call Drew. I doubted there was anything at Peggy's house that would matter. I headed back to the shop. It had been a long morning, and it was barely 11:30. How was that even possible? It seemed like it should've been time to close the shop and go to bed. I was exhausted.

When I got back, I noticed Trevor's car parked out front. I thought that was odd. He had taken the teaching position at the medical college and told me he still had a lot to do before the fall semester began. There were administrative details to be taken care of, plus his preparations for his classes.

He and Emmie seemed to be deep into a conversation, so deep that they didn't even see me walking from the workroom into the front of the store.

"I'm glad she has you," I heard Emmie saying.

"A girl needs great friends," I interjected.

"And someone in this room has great friends," Trevor said.

Emmie just glared at me. She constantly scolded me for the snail's pace my relationship with Trevor was taking, but we had good reasons for it. She also knew that.

"Not that I'm unhappy to see you, but I thought you were swamped today," I said.

"A man has to eat," he replied. "I was hoping to take you out for lunch."

Emmie smiled broadly.

"Just leave this place to me," she said. "I have it covered."

"Anything I need to know?" I asked her.

"I don't think so. We can talk when you get back."

"Are you hungry?" Trevor asked me.

"I don't know. I haven't really thought about it."

"Just as I thought," he said as he turned to walk out the door. I followed him.

"You two have fun," Emmie called.

I ignored her comment. I noticed a cooler in the back seat of his car when I got in.

"Picnic?" I asked as he started the car.

"For a June day, it's not too humid or hot yet."

I laughed.

"Are you sure about that? Yes, we're having a cold spell. It's only supposed to be 90 today," I answered sarcastically.

"Better than 98," he winked. "Besides, there are a lot of trees where we're going. I just needed to get out of that building."

"Shade will definitely help. Do I get any other clues?"

"I was thinking Pendleton King Park."

Pendleton King Park was a 64-acre tract in the heart of Augusta. Its one-time owner was John Pendleton King, a senator in the 1800s who was influential in developing the Georgia Railroad, Georgia Railroad Bank, and the Augusta Canal. He willed the property to his son, Henry, and daughter-in-law, Elizabeth. They had a son, John Pendleton King II, who was called Pendleton. He was a writer and poet who served as an Army liaison officer in World War I. Only three weeks after returning to Augusta from the war, he heard screams coming from Lake Elizabeth on the grounds of the estate. Two women were drowning; he saved one of them, but the other died. Not long after that, Pendleton, who was only 29, became ill and died. They think it was a brain aneurysm. When Henry Pendleton died, he stipulated in his will that the property be used as a bird sanctuary.

It was developed into a park in the 1960s. Over the years, other improvements have been made including the addition of a bark park, a disc golf course and two playgrounds. The park has a beautiful gazebo, a hydrangea garden, and a camellia garden. There are tons of trees and lots of green space. It's a true city gem with many civic organizations adopting it to beautify and maintain it.

"Where would you like to sit?" he asked after parking.

"Did you bring a blanket?"

"As a matter of fact, I did."

"The picnic tables are crowded today."

"Then let's find a spot near some trees," he said.

That was easy enough. Depending on where you were, the park had plenty of trees, and they all had lush green leaves this time of year. Despite being a weekday, the park was busy because school was out. There were groups of toddlers and adults, which I assumed to be a playgroup of some sort; several people playing disc golf. Not only is Augusta a mecca for traditional golf fans, but disc golf has a home in the area with the Professional Disc Golf Association headquartered nearby.

While some people were throwing discs for their dogs, others had their furry friends on leashes at the nearby bark park.

"It's not too exciting. Chicken salad, grapes, crackers, some bottled water," he said, opening the cooler.

"It's food, and I haven't had anything to eat today."

"I hear you've had an exciting morning," he raised an eyebrow as he opened the chicken salad. A light breeze began to blow ruffling his blonde curls.

I pushed my hair behind my ears.

"Yeah, I guess you could say that. It's been nonstop since about 3:30 this morning. I knew you had a busy day, too, and I didn't want to bother you."

I glanced away when I said that.

"But you called Emmie."

"Yeah, I called Emmie at the ungodly hour for a couple of

reasons. First, I knew Drew would be coming for a visit. I didn't want to be alone with him, and I didn't want you there because I didn't want any drama."

"Drama? Me?" he laughed. Sunlight glinted in his blue eyes, but his smile didn't quite reach them. I knew this job and his brothers were causing him a lot of unnecessary stress, and it showed.

"You know what I mean. He doesn't need to know what's going on in my personal life. If you were there … let's just say I didn't want to open the door for any questions. Emmie didn't have the boys or else I wouldn't have called."

He tilted his head and stared at me.

"What?" I asked.

"Are you okay?"

I spooned some of the chicken salad out of the container and put it on a cracker.

"I just saw Jimmy last night. How could he be gone? And why was I one of the last people to see him alive?"

Cold chicken salad tasted good on such a day. There was a light breeze blowing as we sat beneath the shade trees.

"And then this morning, I saw Peggy because I had to deliver flowers to her," I continued. "She's as much of a mess as I expected her to be."

"So, how are you in all of this? Another case of feeling like you should've done more?"

Tears started to well in my eyes. He was right. He'd gone straight to the heart of it. I should've done something. I should've called Drew or Peggy myself. I shouldn't have relied on someone else to do it for me. I knew things weren't right with Jimmy. I put the food down.

"You're right, Trevor. Absolutely correct," I said with the tears starting to flow. "But even before the dream, I knew something was wrong. I should've done something."

"Grace. You can't save everyone," he said softly. "You had no way of knowing he'd be murdered. People get upset about things all the time. Usually, they turn out to be nothing."

"I know. But this was something this time. Look, let's talk about something else."

Before I could suggest another topic, a golden retriever with a flying disc in his mouth joined our picnic.

"Cooper. Cooper," yelled a 20-something year-old man wearing blue shorts and a white tank top. He rushed up to us.

"Sorry about that. Cooper is trying to trade for some of your lunch," he said, slightly out of breath.

I reached out to touch the dog, who dropped the disc in hopes of a snack. I scratched his silky ears.

"Hey, are you Dr. Blake?" the man asked.

Trevor nodded in affirmation. He extended his hand to Trevor.

"I'm Chris. I'm a medical student. I was on the website yesterday. I've been wondering who Dr. Blake was. I saw your photo. I'll be in your class in the fall."

Trevor smiled as he shook Chris's hand.

"It's nice to meet you, Chris. This is my friend, Grace. What are your goals?"

"I want to specialize in cardiology."

I thought I saw Trevor's eye twitch with that.

"My brother is a cardiologist," he said.

"I've heard a lot of good things about the Doctors Blake in this town. Glad to finally meet one. Listen, I'm sorry to interrupt."

"He's a beautiful dog," I interjected.

Chris knelt down next to Cooper and rubbed his fur.

"Thanks. He's still a puppy. He's my girlfriend's dog. We're trying to train him, but he has a mind of his own. And food is always on it."

"I'm sorry, Cooper. I don't have any puppy treats," I said as I touched him.

"That's okay. I have some treats."

Cooper's ears perked up with the word "treats."

"Glad to know you understand some words," Chris said as he reached into his pocket and pulled out a treat for Cooper, who ate it with gusto.

"I'll see you soon, Chris," Trevor said as Chris began to walk away.

I watched Trevor's face. He seemed lost in thought, and he didn't seem too happy with what was transpiring there.

"Trevor, you really don't want to do this, do you?"

He raised an eyebrow.

"Why do you say that, Grace?"

"You don't seem excited about it."

"Drew is probably right. You should be a detective."

I wrinkled my nose.

"No, I'm just observant and sensitive."

"Dangerous combination. You're also extremely inquisitive."

I smiled.

"I'll take that to mean that I'm right. Trevor, you've tried to pretend, and you have a really good poker face. You almost had me believing that you wanted to take this job, but something has never set well with me about it."

"I can't hide anything from you, can I?" he asked.

"Do you want to?"

"No, I don't want to hide anything from you," he glanced around and shrugged his shoulders. "I really don't know what I want to do, Grace, but I have to do something. I can't sit around the house all day. I need to be productive."

"No, the 'but' is that your brothers pushed you into this."

He took a deep breath before answering.

"You know they made suggestions," he said.

"Yes. I do. They were forceful with their suggestions."

He laughed.

"Grace, I'll be fine. I enjoyed working at the clinic; I do care about people. At the clinic, the stresses that I had before weren't there, but I knew it was only temporary," he said. "This will be a good experience for me. Maybe from this side, I'll understand more of the passion these med students have, and maybe I'll get it back."

I smiled at him. He glanced down.

"Besides, my brothers can finally be proud of me in Augusta. They don't need to be embarrassed that I left my practice in North Carolina," he said sarcastically. "Speaking of my brothers, are you ready for their dog and pony show on Saturday?"

He winked at me. I shook my head "no."

In honor of Trevor's new job, his brothers - or maybe it was his sisters-in-law - had planned a reception at the country club. It started out as just a family dinner but ballooned to include the doctors in the practices the brothers worked in and their plus ones. I think there were a few other family friends invited. I wasn't privy to all the details. Since Beth's husband, Knox, had recently joined the practice with Trevor's brother, Edward, Beth and Knox were invited. I was thrilled at the idea of having Beth there. I wasn't going to be able to hide completely from this crowd, but she would guide me through it. She moved around those types of events with ease. She'd coach me through everything. I couldn't duck out of this one. I knew I needed to be there for Trevor.

"As ready as I'll ever be. Emmie and Jazzy are taking care of flowers for a couple of evening weddings, so Beth and I can be there."

"You'll be fine. I have confidence in you."

I smiled weakly.

"Your brothers don't like me."

"No, that's not completely true. Only Richard doesn't like you, but he doesn't even like me. I doubt he likes anyone. It's funny that he's a cardiologist. I'm surprised he even has a heart."

I laughed, but then felt bad about it. Trevor smiled mischievously.

"Trevor, that's not like you," I tried to admonish him, but we both ended up laughing even more.

"We both know it's true. He's got as much personality as a fence post, and he's never liked me because I was Mama's favorite.

Everyone else, including all three of my sisters-in-law, adore you. You'll be fine."

"Really?" I asked warily.

"Absolutely."

"I'll be there for you, Trevor, but this isn't the sort of event I'd go to unless you were there."

"That's all I ask," he said.

Lunch was over too quickly, and Trevor drove me back to the shop.

"I don't know if I'll be finished in time to see you tonight," he said as he walked me inside.

"I understand. Thank you for lunch."

He smiled as he headed out the door.

7

"You look like you had a good lunch," said Emmie, who left the workroom and the arrangement she'd been working on to be nosy. "Your cheeks are rosy."

Emmie folded her arms against her chest and grinned at me as though she had a secret she didn't want to share. I put my hands on my hips and stared at her.

"It's 90 something degrees outside. I could be sunburned or have a heat rash."

She ignored me.

"Trevor is so romantic," she sighed.

"Yes, he is, Emmie, but we are building a friendship. That's the most important thing," I said. I noticed Emmie rolling her eyes at me as I passed her on my way to the workroom.

"What are you working on, Emmie?"

Emmie followed me and walked over to where she'd been working.

"I got a couple of calls about baby arrangements," she said as she put a few pink carnations in some foam.

"Have you heard anything about Jimmy yet? I haven't paid any attention to my phone."

"Not paying attention to your phone when you are with a handsome doctor is a good thing. But, yes, I saw it on the newspaper's website. It was brief. It just said that a man's body had been found,

45

and it gave the location. It mentioned that it was under investigation. There wasn't much more information. Since I know where Jimmy's shop is, it wasn't difficult to figure out," she said. She put down the pink carnations she was using for the baby arrangement and stared at me. "I can't believe he's gone."

She started to cry. I walked over to her and put my arms around her.

"I know, Emmie. I know. Jimmy wasn't just my best customer. I thought of him as a friend. We saw so much of him over the past few years," I said as I held her tightly. I pulled back after a few moments, and I wiped my own tears away.

"He was always talking about the arrangements I made and how Peggy loved them. It made me feel good," she said.

As we were talking, Beth walked in the storeroom. She had the same stunned look on her face that Emmie had earlier.

"I guess you've heard," Beth said.

"Grace has known longer than most people," Emmie replied.

"What are you talking about?" Beth asked.

"Jimmy came by last night after closing time. We talked for a while and he almost wiped out my refrigerator case again," I said.

"Plus, she had a dream, and Drew was an early morning guest, questioning her and asking for her help," Emmie interjected.

"You saw Drew this morning," Beth queried.

"Yes, I knew he was going to come so I woke Emmie up. She was there with me," I paused. "Beth, does the name Steve Mathis mean anything to you?"

Beth's mouth dropped. I didn't surprise Beth often, but when I did, it was obvious.

"Yes, as a matter of fact. My mother and Peggy go to the same salon. They both go at least twice a month, and they often run into each other. Different hairdressers, but same salon. I was with Mama when we heard the news. She told me that Peggy and Jimmy weren't living together and haven't been for several weeks now."

Now it was my turn to be surprised. I felt my mouth drop.

"What? He was in here last night planning a big birthday party for her. He told me how much he loved her and always had. He insisted they were fine. But he *overly* insisted now that I think about it."

The more I thought about Jimmy the sadder I got.

"Mama said she overheard Peggy talking about the problems she and Jimmy were having," Beth said. "It had a lot to do with money. But Mama said she noticed something about Peggy when she started talking about a dinner she was going to. There was a 'twinkle' in her eyes, and she had a 'girlish giggle.' Twinkle was the word Mama used. She said she could see Peggy's face in the mirror. That twinkle reminded Mama of a woman in love. That rankled Mama because she's known Peggy and Jimmy forever, too."

I sighed.

"Jimmy kept going on and on about how much he loved Peggy. I visited Mama last night because he was acting so strangely. Mama said she'd call Peggy, but she told me this morning she couldn't reach Peggy," I said.

Beth folded her arms across her chest.

"Sounds like there was more than a business meeting taking place last night."

"I can't believe this," Emmie said. "They are the last two I expected to split up."

"Well, they weren't divorced yet, but Mama said Peggy was talking about it. It had to do with money, and Peggy was tired of him 'squandering' theirs. Mama said that's the word Peggy used: 'squandering,'" Beth added.

"Did she mention a man?"

"Not one specifically, but Steve Mathis has lots of money, from what Mama said. Peggy is still a beautiful woman and, apparently, they had a thing years ago."

"That's what Daddy told me," I said. "Peggy? An affair?"

Now it was Emmie's turn to fold her arms against her chest. She looked straight at me and issued a challenge with her next question.

"So, Grace, are you going to call Drew?" Emmie asked.

"Why are you looking at me like that? This is all hearsay."

"It's the exact sort of thing that Drew wanted you to find out for him, and you know it."

"Well, I don't want to talk to Drew."

"If Peggy was having an affair, how would that get Jimmy killed?" I continued. "Seems like Jimmy would be the one doing the killing, and I doubt he'd kill Peggy. He'd be more likely to go after the man. Besides, can you honestly see Peggy shooting someone? She'd break a nail. And those nails were perfect this morning."

Emmie burst out into laughter on that.

"Okay, you might have something on that one, but maybe there was a confrontation," Emmie said. "Maybe he threatened her. Maybe it was self-defense. Maybe this Steve Mathis person wanted to get Jimmy out of the way."

"I don't know. I'm not a detective. That's Drew's area of expertise," I said as I walked out of the workroom and into my office.

"You'll call Drew," she said.

I sat down at my desk. Beth followed me and sat down in the extra chair.

"About Saturday," she started.

I groaned.

"Don't remind me."

Beth laughed.

"Stop being so dramatic," she said. "I have a couple of dresses that would be perfect for this. You need to come to my house and pick one out."

"Do we have to? Could we just skip to Sunday?"

"What are you afraid of?"

"Oh, I don't know, Beth. His brothers hate me, and so do his sisters-in-law."

"No, they don't. I know Trevor's brothers. Knox works with Edward, who is a great doctor. He and James are super nice. Yes,

Richard is difficult, but all the wives are fantastic. I'm in a garden club with Edward's wife, Vivian, and she's as sweet as they come. And James' wife, Claire, is straightforward, but at least she does have tact. When they found out I was your friend, they wanted to know about you. Claire and Vivian think you're quiet, but that you're good for Trevor. I don't know Richard's wife, Nadine, well. So, I can't tell you anything about her."

"Trevor said pretty much the same thing about them liking me."

"Well, there you have it. He's not lying. You know I'd tell you the truth."

"Yes, Beth. I can count on you not to sugar coat something," I said and smiled. "I'm just glad you'll be there."

"I love parties, and this will be fun if you let it. I know your fun side," she said. "Just don't be uptight about it, and you'll be fine."

"I need a cheerleader. I appreciate it."

"I'll see you later. Call me if you need anything, and get over to my house soon to try on these dresses, okay?"

"Sure."

The rest of the day sped by as quickly as the first part. I finally saw a brief article online about Jimmy's suspicious death. Funeral arrangements were pending. That meant I had a little time before the orders came in.

While at my desk, I decided to play a little detective on my own. I did a search for the name "Steve Mathis." I found several people by that name, but one stood out. There was a real estate company in Atlanta under that name. I scrolled through the site until I found information on the company's management. There was a photo of a tall, slender man with snow white hair and a mustache. He wore an expensive-looking suit and a gold watch. His bio said that he was originally from Augusta. I stared at the photo. Why did it say "the Godfather" to me?

That had to be him. He had additional offices in Nashville, Charlotte, and Charleston. There was a little personal information. It mentioned he had three children and four grandchildren, but there was no mention of a wife.

I was pretty sure he was the person investing in whatever Peggy's business venture was, but was there something else? Peggy was a beautiful woman. She paid meticulous attention to her appearance. But if there was something else going on, would that have cost Jimmy his life? I still thought he was afraid of someone or something.

I hadn't paid too much attention to my phone. I did, however, notice missed calls from my mother and Drew. I knew Mama would be upset with me for not telling her about Jimmy.

The store phone rang. I would let Emmie answer it while I finished some paperwork. I heard a knock on the door. Emmie stuck her head in.

"Sweetie, you should know better than to ignore your Mama," she said. "I put her on hold; she's on line one."

"She's going to fuss at me for not telling her about Jimmy, and you know it."

"Then, suck it up. You can't avoid her forever."

"Make an excuse."

"No. I will not."

She turned and went back into the shop.

"Yes, Ms. Lottie, she'll be right with you."

She peeked around the corner and grinned at me.

"Hi, Mama," I said into the phone, trying to be perky.

"You're ignoring me."

"I'm working. I'm not ignoring you."

"How could you not tell me about Jimmy?" she didn't sound angry. It was more hurt.

I took a deep breath.

"I didn't want to believe it, Mama. I still don't believe it."

"I should've done more," she said.

"No, Mama. You can't blame yourself. You told me you called Peggy; that's all you could've done."

"I don't know. I could've called a couple of times instead of just once."

"Beating yourself up won't bring him back, Mama."

As I said those words, I realized where I got my tendencies from, or *who* I got them from, rather. That was definitely something she'd passed on to me.

"I think you're wrong, Grace."

"What could you have possibly done differently?"

"I don't know."

"Then there's your answer. Nothing you would've done could've helped."

I was itching to ask her some questions, but I could hear the tears in her voice. She was shaken and asking about Jimmy and Peggy's marital status wouldn't help that situation. I was bracing myself for her to ask me a question.

"I guess I'll be making some lemon pound cakes. I'll make one for you to take to Trevor if you'd like."

"Trevor won't eat a whole pound cake," I laughed.

"Did I hear someone say 'pound cake?'" Emmie bounded into my office like a kid waiting to give Santa her wish list. "I'll take some of Miss Lottie's pound cake."

"Did you hear that?" I asked. "Emmie wants pound cake if you're offering."

Mama started laughing.

"Tell her I'll make one for her and her boys."

"She'll make you one," I relayed the message to Emmie.

"I can't wait. Thanks, Mrs. B," she said as she went back to work.

"I need to go," I said. I wanted her off the phone before she could ask me about Drew.

"Not so fast. Have you seen Drew Ward?"

Just when I thought I'd gotten away from that subject. I hesitated before answering that, and it wasn't lost on my mother.

"Drew is a homicide investigator, and he happens to be working this case," was my lame answer.

"So that's a 'yes.'"

"Well. I think it was pretty much unavoidable."

"Humph," she scoffed at me. "Are you helping him?"

She couldn't see my face, but she was my mother. Even on the phone, she'd know if I was lying; apparently a lie made a different sound. What that sound was I couldn't tell you, but it was different. I tried to avoid answering it.

"Drew came to my apartment early this morning. I was one of the last people to see Jimmy alive. Of course, I've talked to him."

"No, that's not what I asked. But you just told me everything I needed to know. I can't believe you're going to help him. Not after everything he's put you through."

"Mama, I never said I was going to help him, and you're the one who always taught me about forgiving people."

"Forgiving someone is one thing. Continuing to help them is another. Come by in the morning, and I'll have your pound cake. Goodbye, Grace," she said as she hung up.

I couldn't win for losing on this one, but I was determined to find out what had happened to Jimmy, even if that meant I had to talk to Drew.

A few minutes before four, I got a phone call to deliver an order to Jimmy's shop. I thought it was strange. Shouldn't his shop be closed?

"Are you sure you don't want it delivered to his home or the funeral home?" I asked the caller.

"No. His business," the caller replied.

"I'll get it over there in the next hour," I said before ending the call.

"What was that about?" Emmie asked.

"Someone wants us to deliver a funeral wreath to Jimmy's business."

"Not the funeral home?"

"That's what I asked, but he said he wanted it to go there. It's J&M automotive parts in Columbia."

"Any specific flowers?"

"No. He just said to use your judgement."

"Are you going to take it over there?" she asked.

"Yes."

"I'd be happy to go with you."

"Thanks, Emmie. I can't imagine that anyone will be there. Would you mind closing up?"

"Not at all.

I took the wreath and packed it into my car. I didn't expect anyone to be there, but when I pulled up, there was one vehicle outside. It wasn't Jimmy's or Peggy's.

Wasn't this still a crime scene? No one should've been working there. I got out of my car with the arrangement and walked to the office door. It was unlocked, and there wasn't a bell or an alarm to signal my presence. I slipped into the building carrying the wreath. The auto shop was a large, windowless metal building with a glass door. Inside, there was a small waiting area with two vending machines, a worn leather couch, and a coffee table strewn with magazines and days-old newspapers. Several empty office desks were behind the counter. There were two enclosed offices and a door that led to the garage. One of those offices had bright yellow police tape across its doorway. I couldn't imagine what that office must look like, and I didn't want to try. I was sure it hadn't been cleaned yet. The door was open, and the light was on. I couldn't see into the room, but I could hear a woman's voice.

"This wasn't supposed to happen, Billy," she said. "He wasn't supposed to die."

Her voice sounded familiar. I couldn't hear anyone reply. She must've been on the phone. My heart started pounding. Why was Debbie in Jimmy's office? What was she looking for?

"I'm getting it now. I hid it in a place even the police won't find it, but we've got to get out of town soon. I have to check Jimmy's office to make sure he didn't leave anything else."

I rushed back outside. I leaned against the brick wall and tried to catch my breath. I wondered what she was talking about. I had to go back inside. I counted to 20. I took a deep breath and opened the door. This time I called out.

"Hello? Debbie? Is anyone here?"

Debbie was his longtime office manager/bookkeeper, and I was sure it was her voice that I'd heard.

She peeked out of Jimmy's office with her phone in her hand. She was in her 50s. She had bright red hair, which Emmie and I had decided had to have come out of a bottle. She kept it in the same poufy hair style she'd had since the late 1980s. I was pretty sure there was a hole in the ozone layer because of all the hair spray she'd used in 35 years. She also wore the same makeup, and her lipstick matched her nail polish all the time. She had her phone in her hand and hastily pushed it into the pocket of her skinny jeans.

"Grace," she smiled and pretended to be happy to see me. She wasn't a good actress.

"Hi," I said in my equally pretend perky voice. "I wasn't sure anyone would be here, but I got a call from a parts supplier. J&M in Columbia. He insisted I bring this here to the shop, not to the funeral home."

Her smile vanished and her jaw clenched when I mentioned the name of the supplier.

"It's lovely. I'll hang it on the door. We really should have something like that to let people know we're closed for a death."

She reached over the counter, and I saw traces of blood on her hands. I tried not to gag as I saw her hands. I stared at them as she pulled the wreath to her side of the counter. She barely blinked an eye at me. I couldn't believe how callous she was. Her statement hit me. They were supposed to be closed. If they were closed, why was she there? She didn't offer me any explanation.

"It's good of you to drop by. I'm sure I'll see you at the funeral."

I wasn't going to be dismissed that easily.

"Of course, Jimmy was one of my favorite customers."

"Jimmy was a good man. This is so sad," she said, but her expression didn't match her words. There was no hint of sadness. She didn't look like she'd shed a single tear for the man who employed her for three decades. What I did see was that same look of fear in her eyes that I'd seen in Jimmy's the night before.

I forced a fake smile.

"But yes, I'm sure I'll see you at the funeral." I said as I turned to walk out the door.

I got into my car and drove a few blocks away so I could pull into a crowded parking lot to call Drew. My heart was still beating wildly, and my hands shook as I took the phone out of my purse.

"Ignoring my calls?" he answered in a snarky tone.

"Stop, just stop, okay," my voice was just shy of hysterical. Seeing Jimmy's blood on Debbie's hands and her lack of emotion had pushed me over the edge. "I had to drop a wreath off at Jimmy's shop, and Debbie was there. She didn't hear me come in at first. I overheard her on the phone with someone named Billy saying she was looking for something and that Jimmy wasn't supposed to die."

My voice broke.

"Drew, she had blood on her hands," I started to cry. I took in a deep breath and tried to continue. "She said she'd hidden it so even the police couldn't find it. I left and then came back trying to make as much noise as I could so she wouldn't think I'd been there. I talked to her. I don't want her to know I was the one who tipped you off."

"Don't worry, Grace. Are you okay?"

"No, Drew. I'm not okay. How can I be? She had smears of Jimmy's blood on her hands like it was no big deal. I think I need to throw up or cry or something."

"I understand. With your help, we can find who did this. That won't make everything okay, but it will help us get justice for him."

"I'm not sure I can handle this."

"Grace, you're an amazing woman, and you've handled more than a lot of people I know."

I took a deep breath.

"Thank you, Drew."

"Good night, Grace."

8

After I ended my call with Drew, I drove home. With Emmie closing up for me, I made it home before actual closing time, but I was exhausted. I wasn't used to being up at 3 a.m. Not that I'd slept before then anyway. I'd never functioned well on limited sleep. Drew always amazed me. He could go for long stretches without sleep, but not me. I needed those eight or more hours. I supposed Trevor was the same. Doctors often went for long stretches without sleep. I guess he'd learned how to do that as well. When I got inside my garage apartment, I sent Trevor a text thanking him again for lunch and telling him I was wiped out and needed sleep. He said he understood, but he and his mother's rose garden missed me. I did need to make a trip to the rose garden. It was coming back to its former glory, and I loved every second of it.

I took a quick shower and put on a pair of comfortable shorts and a tank top.

I fried a couple of pieces of bacon and had a bacon and tomato sandwich slathered with mayonnaise. Trevor made me eat more of a health-conscious diet most of the time, but since he wasn't with me, I was taking full advantage, and I was going to enjoy every last savory bite of it.

I sat down on my couch with my juicy sandwich and a glass of ice-cold sweet tea, taking time between each bite.

It had been the first time I'd sat down since my impromptu

picnic with Trevor. After finishing the sandwich, I leaned back and closed my eyes. I didn't intend to fall asleep there.

The sound of someone knocking on the door roused me from my nap. I was disoriented and had no idea what time it was when I woke up. I dragged myself to the door. I opened to see Drew.

"I tried calling," he said as he stood at the door holding a large cup with a straw in it. It was still light outside, which meant I couldn't have slept that long. Or was it the next morning? I touched my forehead and frowned at him.

"I fell asleep. What time is it anyway?" I asked as I rubbed my face.

"About 8:30."

"P.M.?" I asked. "What day is it?"

He chuckled.

"That must've been some nap," he said. "Yes, p.m., and it's still Tuesday."

I yawned.

"This has been the absolute longest day of my life," I said.

"Can I come in?" he asked. "It's hot out here."

He smiled at me as he held out the cup.

"Is that for me?"

"Yes, you extended your Southern hospitality to me this morning. I thought I'd return the favor."

I knew it had to be sweet tea, and that sounded heavenly about now. I took it from him and stepped back, allowing him in. I stared at the cup, wondering why he was making a house call. I knew it wasn't to bring me sweet tea.

"Thank you."

"Listen, I wanted to apologize for this morning," he started.

I glanced up at him. Since I was still trying to wake up, I wasn't exactly sure what he was talking about. It seemed liked weeks had passed since the morning. I furrowed my brow and shrugged my shoulders without saying anything.

"I guess instinct kicked in," he said.

"I don't follow."

"When you started crying, my first thought was to hold you. I guess I shouldn't have done that, and I upset you even more when I called you 'babe.' It's a habit that I need to break."

I didn't respond right away but stared at the floor. He was right; it was a natural thing to just let him hold me as I cried. It was the "babe" that hurt.

"Yes, there were times when I wasn't sure if my first name was 'Grace' or if it was 'Babe.'" I tried to laugh, but it sounded more like a grunt.

"No Emmie?"

"No," I closed the door and walked into the space. It was obvious he wasn't leaving. "She's got the boys tonight."

"Ah."

There was an awkward silence.

"Grace, you look really good," he said.

I wasn't sure how to respond to that. I was too tired to be mad at him even though I probably should've been.

"Thank you. Trevor makes me eat better, and I've started exercising more."

"The good Dr. Blake."

His timbre changed with that. His voice was soft when he said I looked good, but it turned cold with the mention of Trevor's name.

I smiled and folded my arms against my chest.

"Is this a personal call, Drew?"

"Not really, but if it was, would you be happy to see me?" he asked.

"I'm not unhappy to see you right now, if that's what you're asking. I just only see you under less-than-desirable circumstances."

He nodded to agree with me on that statement.

"Like I said, I've tried to call you several times today."

He was right. I'd ignored a few calls during the day. I walked over to the table and picked up my phone. There were two missed calls during my nap. And then there were the other calls. I didn't tell him everything when I'd called earlier.

"I did call you once," I offered with a faint smile and a shrug.

"True, but I couldn't talk long then, and I was wondering if you had anything else for my case," he continued.

I should've called him and then we could've avoided all this. I did have things I wanted to tell him.

"I knew I needed to call you, but my workday was crazy busy. When I got home, I crashed on my couch as you can see."

"Did you record anything else?"

I laughed.

"No, I didn't, but I did make a few notes on my phone."

I walked over to the kitchen table and sat down. Drew followed my lead. I relayed to him the events of the day from my meeting with my mother and the later phone call, my internet search on Steve Mathis, Beth's mother's gossip about Peggy, my visit to Peggy's, and just about everything else except my lunch with Trevor. My notes included my observations of the way people acted around me.

Drew had few facial expressions as I talked, but I knew he was taking in everything that I said.

"And you weren't going to call me?" he asked in an aggravated tone.

"Some of it is just hearsay."

"Hearsay is only a problem in court, but in my investigation, it helps to point me in the right direction – just like your dreams do," he said, meeting my eyes.

I broke the uncomfortable gaze and glanced at my phone.

"Did you already know all of this?"

"Actually, no. Peggy didn't tell me that she and Jimmy weren't living together. I don't know where he was living. The shop didn't look like someone was staying there. He did have a couch in his office, but there was no pillow or blankets or other signs of anyone sleeping there. We looked."

"An affair with this Steve Mathis character makes her look awfully suspicious, doesn't it?" I asked.

He shrugged his shoulders.

"Drew, do you really think Peggy could kill someone? I mean, this is Peggy Hughes we're talking about."

"I never thought Dana Andrews would kill anyone either and look how that turned out."

"I guess you're right," I said as I fumbled to think of anything else to say.

The brief silence was awkward.

"Peggy's fingernails were perfectly manicured when I was there this morning. I don't think she was firing any guns," I offered.

"I haven't completely ruled her out just yet," he said blandly.

One thing that had bothered me all day was how my mother had reacted to me.

"What's the matter, Grace?"

"My mother."

"Lottie?"

"Yes. She never snaps at me, but when I went to get those flowers, I asked her if the name of Steve Mathis meant anything, and she shut me down. She told me she wasn't a gossip, which makes me think she knows more than she's telling me."

"You're right. I've never seen Lottie snap. She's always been as sweet as that tea you're drinking."

"And she didn't know that Jimmy was dead when I went over there this morning. I didn't have the heart to tell her. She finally tracked me down, and she wasn't too happy with me when she found out I knew and said nothing. She started asking me questions and that made her even more upset."

"Questions like if you're helping me with my investigation?" I laughed.

"How did you know, Drew?" I asked sarcastically.

"What did you tell her?"

"Some partial truths. I told her you'd interviewed me since I was one of the last people to see him."

"And?"

I laughed.

"And she said I answered her question. She wasn't happy about it at all. She's not happy with you."

"I know, Grace. A lot of people aren't happy with me. But that sounds like your mom. What did you tell Trevor?"

When he said "Trevor," I noticed him glance down at my hands which I'd folded in front of me on the table. I was sure he was taking in the bare left hand. I really didn't want to have that conversation with him again. I moved my hands to my lap.

"What do you mean, Drew?"

"About helping me with my investigation."

"He and I aren't dating. I don't tell him everything. I don't tell anyone everything," I glared at him when I said that. "As far as helping your investigation, I didn't tell him anything, and he didn't ask. He's got a lot of other things on his mind right now. He's starting a new job teaching at the medical college."

"I could see him doing that," Drew said with a smile. "Professor Dr. Blake. It fits."

"I thought you weren't here to talk about my personal life. Besides, you didn't ask me to help with your investigation. You asked me to help Jimmy," I locked eyes with him on that part. I wanted him to know my motivation wasn't to help Drew. "You just asked me to feed you any information that I might come across in my regular business."

"Yes, Grace. I want you as an informant, not a detective," he said as he maintained that eye contact with me. We were in a battle of wills. We both knew each other too well, and we both knew one of the reasons I wanted to solve the case had nothing to do with Drew or Jimmy. I'd started to enjoy unraveling these mysteries. That scared me in a way. With each case, I'd gotten a little bolder; a little less afraid of putting myself in a possibly dangerous situation just so I could find the answers we were looking for. "If anything happened to you, I'd never forgive myself. I've put you in harm's way too many times."

The last sentence came as a faint whisper. It was the tone, not the words that shook me. The look he gave me along with it was one I'd seen after I'd suffered a miscarriage. It was a look of compassion and helplessness. It was the look of wanting to make everything right in my world but feeling powerless to do it at the same time. It was a look I was familiar with, and I was surprised to see it. I could only imagine the expression on my face. I broke our gaze, trying to ignore that remark. I desperately tried to think of something else to say.

"One thing doesn't add up in this to me, Drew."

"And that is?"

"Why was Jimmy so scared last night? He wasn't scared of Peggy. I mean maybe he was scared of losing her, but in my shop, he was jittery. He kept looking out the window, and he insisted on going into my office, which is something he never does. He even parked out back; that's something else he never does."

"I'm sure you're right on that one."

"And when I talked to Debbie and mentioned where the wreath had come from, she had that same look on her face."

"That's interesting," he said and tilted his head to the side.

"Did you find out what she was looking for in the office?"

"No, we didn't. Someone stopped by to do a check on the crime scene, and the deputy stayed until she left. She didn't have anything with her."

"I wonder if it was whatever he had in those file folders."

"That's possible."

"Did you find out who she was talking to, Drew?" I asked.

"Billy? When the officer went to the shop and checked on her, he also checked the last number dialed out of the office. It was to a Billy Jeffries. He is one of the mechanics who works there."

"One of the mechanics. Could he have killed Jimmy?'

"I'm working on it, Grace."

"Are you going to tell me anything else, Drew?"

He smiled.

"There's really nothing to tell you at this point. We don't have any real suspects right now. There are no security cameras at his shop. We're looking into the financials at both his business and his home. I'm checking into Debbie too. I don't know what she was after or what she's hiding, but we'll find out. I'll also check into that parts supplier. We'll exhaust every avenue to find his killer. I will promise you that. The autopsy should be finished soon, and then Peggy can go forward with his funeral. When that happens, you'll be busy and will find yourself in places where you can listen in on conversations and watch people."

"I agreed to do that."

"I know, and I appreciate it," he said.

He leaned back in the chair and folded his arms against his chest. He furrowed his brow as though he was thinking of something but wasn't sure what to say.

"What's the matter, Drew?"

"Nothing is the matter. Tell me, Grace, what do you think?"

What did I think? When was that ever something he cared about concerning a case? I eyed him suspiciously.

"What do you mean, Drew?"

He shrugged his shoulders.

"This case. What do you think? Where is your internet search later going to take you?" he asked that last question with a mischievous grin.

I paused to think about an answer. I knew exactly what I wanted to search for on the internet, but I was sure I wouldn't find it. It had to do with that business that had called the flowers in.

"Honestly, Debbie would be at the top of my list. She's hiding something. I don't know what she did, but I guarantee you, it was either illegal or immoral. Maybe a little of both. I don't see Peggy as a murderer. They'd been together for 30 years; she may have been trying to divorce him. That would be Peggy's style. Divorce him and take him for every penny he had and more."

Drew chuckled.

"I can agree with that. What else, Grace?"

The fact that he was asking my opinion was unnerving. Why did he even care what I thought? Who was this man?

"Well, who is this Steve Mathis? I've never heard of him before, but everyone in my mother's generation knows him. The business that sent the wreath. I'd be checking on it. You should've seen Debbie's face when I mentioned it. I don't know if she's in cahoots with them or what. But there's something going on there that's deeper than we both see."

I glanced at the table. Drew stared at me and smiled as I continued with my list. I paused.

"Keep going, Grace."

"You know something else that bothered me was how Jimmy's daughter reacted. I watched her. She didn't look sad. She looked angry. Her jaw was set, and there was a fire in her eyes when she said that the business was more important to her father than she was."

"Interesting," he said. "Anything else?"

"Yeah, there's something that has bothered me for a while."

"What?"

"I know he'd joke about it, but I think he had some problems with gambling. His poker games were always getting him into trouble."

Drew's mouth dropped.

"What did I say?"

"You're starting to think like me, and that scares me," he said.

"Why?"

"Because you're right. Things haven't added up in a long time when it comes to Jimmy. I think he's got some skeletons in his closet that are getting ready to come out. It's going to look like Halloween in June."

He glanced at his phone.

"I need to go," he said as he stood and walked to the door. I followed him so I could put the deadbolt on after I let him out.

At the door, he paused and turned to me.

"Grace, have you eaten anything tonight?"

It seemed simple enough. Just a question, so I blurted out the answer.

"My mother had some amazing tomatoes in her garden, and I had a bacon and tomato sandwich earlier. I have a couple of extra tomatoes if you'd like some. Why?"

His eyes locked with mine again as he opened his mouth to say something. He paused, glanced at the floor and then looked back at me.

"No reason, Grace. My mom has a garden full of tomatoes, so I'll pass. Thanks for the offer. I'm – I'm glad you are taking care of yourself. Sleep well."

I watched him go down the stairs, and I closed the door. I played the words over in my head a couple of times. I didn't realize what he was asking at first. He wasn't checking to see if I was taking care of myself even though I had a habit of being too busy and skipping meals. I had a feeling I knew what he was going to say. He was going to ask me to have dinner with him.

I wasn't sure how I felt about that even though my relationship with Trevor wasn't a romantic one. I thought I was getting over Drew. I didn't mind living alone. The introvert in me loved the alone time. I'd gotten plenty of it when I was married to Drew. His work kept him away from me. But deep down I was lonely. I missed being married, having someone there at the end of the day, even if the end of the day was 1 a.m. I just didn't want that loneliness to push me into another relationship. I knew I had feelings for Trevor. I knew I was in love with him and had been for a while, but something still held me back. Even though Drew and I were divorced, the words "til death us do part" still rang in my head. Neither of us were dead. I couldn't completely separate from him, and I didn't dare tell anyone that. I only let my therapist in so far. As I'd told Drew, I didn't tell anyone everything.

I was still tired, but I didn't' think I'd be able to sleep. If

Zack hadn't been out of town on Army business, I would've expected another knock on the door. It was quiet, and tonight the quiet was unnerving. I changed clothes and headed to the grocery store. I wandered down the aisles trying to think of something. I stared at the products until I made my way into the frozen food section. Ice cream – my comfort food. The thing was I never binge ate alone. It had to be with Emmie. I pulled a carton of chocolate chip cookie dough ice cream out of the freezer and put it in the basket. This needed toppings so I wandered until I found the chocolate syrup and the chocolate chips.

When I got in my car, I debated driving to Emmie's. The only person who knew most of my inner thoughts was Emmie, and even she didn't know everything.

I got lost in thought as I turned on my car. Muscle memory led me to Emmie's house, and I sat outside for several minutes before I got out. She was waiting on me at the door, wearing a cute kimono style robe. I didn't say anything; I simply pulled the ice cream out of the bag and held it up.

"Grace, you had me up at 3 a.m. and now it's almost 11."

"I know, but you know you really want some chocolate chip cookie dough ice cream. And if you were really that tired, you'd be in bed instead of watching a movie with a box of tissues."

She folded her arms against her chest.

"You do know I just started keto, right?"

"Fine. I can eat this all by myself; just let me in, will you?'

She stepped back. She'd paused the movie she'd been watching.

"Anything interesting?" I asked.

"No, but I've heard it's a multiple tissue box movie. I just haven't gotten into it yet, sweetie."

"I'll eat my ice cream and leave. I can't watch that."

I walked into her kitchen and pulled a spoon out of the drawer.

"Only one?" she asked.

"I thought you just started keto."

"I did, but I'm starving."

I laughed as I pulled two bowls from her cupboard and another spoon from the drawer.

"You bought the premium stuff and extra chocolate chips," she said. "This must be serious."

I didn't look at her. It had been one super-long day, and I really needed a good cry.

"You've pulled plenty of all-nighters before. What's one more?"

"Well, sweetie. I was young, unemployed, and childless then," Emmie said as she took a spoon and started to dip her own ice cream.

"You're still young," I countered.

She didn't respond but continued to scoop the ice cream, and then she delved into the bag of chocolate chips, eating a few before dropping them on top. I took my decadent bowl of chocolate to the couch, where I sat among the pillows.

Emmie followed.

"So, are we watching a movie, too?"

I'd scooped a heaping spoonful of ice cream just as she said that. I savored every frosty minute of it before I swallowed.

"Your company is enough."

"Wow, this is really bad," she said as she sat down next to me. She folded her legs and turned toward me. "What has happened in the five hours since I last saw you? Was there anyone at Jimmy's shop?"

"Debbie was there, and she didn't seem the least bit upset that Jimmy was dead. I think she's worked for him for 30 years."

"I've never liked that woman."

Emmie's response surprised me.

"Really? Why?"

"Every year on her birthday and on administrative professional's day, Jimmy sends her an arrangement. And every year on those two dates, I deliver it. She barely acknowledges me when

I come in and immediately dismisses me. She waves her hand and tells me to 'put it over there' without even looking. And these are arrangements that I made. Not that anyone else's are bad, but I'm used to people taking notice of my work. I put a lot of emotion and effort into it, and to be dismissed without a proper gushing of how great I've done is totally unacceptable. She's not a nice woman," Emmie said that without a hint of sarcasm.

I wanted to laugh. Emmie did put her heart and soul into her work, and people did gush when she made an arrangement. It wasn't completely out of ego that she said that.

"I didn't realize that about her."

"Oh, and there's more, Grace. I heard she'd taken several pricey vacations over the past year, and she moved into a new house on the river – alone."

"How can she afford that?"

"That's what I want to know, sweetie."

"Who told you all of that?"

"Please, Grace, I don't give up my sources," she said and laughed at me.

"Well, when I walked in, I overheard her talking on the phone to someone. She didn't know I was there. She was looking for something in Jimmy's office. I called Drew."

"Ah, now I know what - . No, I know *who* your problem is," she smiled, seemingly proud of herself for figuring out my problem.

I ignored her and kept going.

"Debbie is up to something, Emmie."

Emmie sighed and rolled her eyes.

"Fine, don't answer. But do you think she killed Jimmy?"

"Maybe? Like I said, I called Drew to let him know that she was at the shop."

"Is that all? What else happened with Drew because I know a phone call didn't warrant chocolate chip cookie dough ice cream," she said.

"He came by my apartment tonight. I'd fallen asleep, and I

was out of it when I woke up. He was at my door with a large sweet tea."

"The way to Grace's heart," Emmie said and laughed.

"He had tried to call, but I was dead. I didn't hear the phone. Anyway, he apologized for hugging me this morning."

She raised an eyebrow at me.

"Yeah, Emmie. Drew apologized for holding me and calling me 'babe.' He told me everything was going to be all right."

"I saw you push him away."

"Drew said he noticed I was upset."

"So, he apologized."

"He did. We talked. He wanted to know everything I'd found out during the day. I can't believe how much information on a case falls into my lap, and I don't even do anything half the time."

"I know, sweetie. Who would've thought a florist would be a detective?"

"Not this florist. That's for sure. I was completely happy with Drew being the crime solver in the family."

"Is that all that happened, sweetie? That doesn't seem like something that would drive you to chocolate overload."

I pursed my lips.

"He wanted to know what I'd do next if I was in his position. He wanted to know what my internet search would be tonight. And then before he left, I think he almost asked me out."

Emmie furrowed her brow and wrinkled her nose.

"Drew almost asked you out?" she repeated.

"Yes, I think so. Of course, he asked about Trevor. He kept staring at my left hand. I don't know why he seems to think I'm just going to jump into marrying someone else," I paused causing Emmie to raise an eyebrow. "It's probably nothing."

"If it was nothing, you and I would both be asleep in our own beds right about now."

"Before he left, he asked if I'd eaten. I was still dazed from my nap and didn't really think about it. I told him I'd had a bacon-and-tomato sandwich, then he started acting weird, and he said 'never mind.' It was just the way he looked at me. At one point, he thanked me for the information and told me one more time that he only wanted me to eavesdrop because if anything happened to me, he'd never forgive himself."

"Like he hasn't put you in danger before. He's full of himself. He almost cost you your life a couple of times. That crazy woman could've killed you. And she tried twice," Emmie's voice began to rise.

She gritted her teeth and shook her head as her breathing became more rapid. She was not happy with Drew. She started to say something else but stopped.

"What is it?" I asked.

"This morning. When we were listening to the recording from last night. You already knew what Jimmy was going to say, so you avoided eye contact with Drew, but when Jimmy said how stupid Drew was for divorcing you, you should've seen Drew's face. It was like a punch to the gut. He winced and closed his eyes briefly. When he looked up, his eyes sparkled like there were tears."

"Don't tell me that, Emmie."

She ignored me and kept talking.

"Funny thing – Drew told me that same thing after he gave me his death glare. He mouthed 'don't' and looked at you."

"Drew's glare of death," I said and tried to laugh. I haven't been on the other end of that in quite a while. If he told you not to tell me, then why did you?"

"Because he crushed your heart, sweetie, and I wanted you to know that he's suffering," Emmie snapped. I knew Emmie was angry with him, but she didn't always verbalize it. Today I was getting more than I bargained for.

I didn't say anything. I looked down at the ice cream; I'd lost my appetite.

"I don't want anyone to suffer. I'm over Drew, Emmie."

Emmie laughed at me.

"You're a horrible liar, Ms. Ward. If you are so over him, then why are you eating all that sugar on my couch at almost midnight on a school night?"

I didn't answer, so she continued.

"Besides, if you really were over him, you and Trevor would be officially dating, and you'd probably have a huge rock on that left hand. You might even be married to him, but I expect he's going to want a wedding – and a big one at that – if for no other reason than to say to all of Augusta that he's married the woman he always wanted to."

"Emmie, that's not something I want to discuss with you."

"Oh no, sweetie, you're the one who started it this time," Emmie was beyond stirred up. She started funneling that anger toward me. "You're the one who came to my house with more calories than anyone should eat in a week when we both should be asleep. You're the one who wants a shoulder to cry on. That's never been a problem, but you're not going to shut me down this time. I will get all of this out of my system."

I stared at her. She'd put down her bowl, folded her arms across her chest, and stared back at me. I could do this, too. I put my bowl down on the coffee table and threw a pillow at her.

"A pillow fight won't get you out of talking to me, Grace," she said as she threw it back at me.

"Trevor wanted me to go to therapy before we started dating. You know that."

"Well, you have been, haven't you?"

"Some. It's expensive, and I didn't realize our policy didn't have mental health coverage. So, I limit my visits or cancel appointments outside of the 24-hour period, so I don't get charged."

Emmie tilted her head.

"I thought Trevor was going to help you pay for it."

"No. I mean, he offered, but I'm not taking his money. I'm an adult. I pay my own bills."

"Fine, but -"

"No, buts, Emmie. I'm paying for it. Besides, Trevor has been so preoccupied with the new job. He really hasn't had much time for me. That's the reason I was so surprised to see him at lunch."

"He seemed fine to me."

"I know. He hides his feelings well. He's been trained to do that just like Drew has.. Trevor's letting his brothers bully him, I think. He doesn't want to admit it. And when I'm with him, he's far away."

"Aw, sweetie. I'm so sorry," she said as she leaned over to give me a hug.

"He's a wonderful friend, but right now, he doesn't even talk about anything else. He used to talk about his plans. At one time, he talked about a future – with me. He'd wink and smile at me, but he stopped doing that when I started going to counseling. We talk about nothing most days – if we talk. We used to have meaningful conversations; now they are shallow. Like I said, he's been really busy lately, and sometimes I just get a text or a call right before I go to sleep. We don't even eat together every day anymore."

I could feel a few tears running down my cheeks. Emmie's face fell as she listened.

"Why didn't you tell me any of this?" Emmie whispered.

"Because you'd tell me 'I told you so.' You'd tell me I was pushing him away."

"Oh sweetie, I'm sorry," she reached out and gave me a hug. "I swear I'll kill the next man to hurt you and if that's Trevor Blake, I'll do it."

I smiled at her.

"You'd be right if you told me 'I told you so.' I did push him away, but my heart couldn't handle the pain. I'm still thinking that Trevor might decide he doesn't want to be with me, especially now."

"But he still wants to see you?"

"Sometimes."

"Do you think there's someone else?"

I shrugged my shoulders.

"No. I'm just hoping he's preoccupied. If he had found

someone else, I don't think he'd still be talking to me. I think he would've told me and ended our friendship. That's the kind of man he is. I do know that much."

"Grace, he asked you to go to that family thing this weekend. He still wants you in his life."

"He did, but he started acting strangely when he found out he'd gotten the job. When his brothers planned this event, he got more nervous. I'm not sure what's going on, and he doesn't really talk about it much."

"Sweetie, I think you're overreacting and overthinking. You're exhausted. It's been one rollercoaster of a day. I think if you get some sleep, you'll see that you're right about thinking Trevor is just preoccupied. I saw his face this morning when he came to take you to lunch. His face lights up like the sky with fireworks on the Fourth of July when he sees you. That man is in love with you. How do you feel about him?"

I knew how I felt, but saying the words out loud was hard.

"You know how I feel about him, Emmie."

"But you can't say it – not even to me?"

I hesitated. I bit my lip before I could utter the words.

"I love him, too, Emmie."

"And Drew?"

"I would've made it work with him, but he pushed me away. He told me he didn't want to be with me, and he told me to get on with my life. I can't take any more pain from him. One of the things I've had to do was forgive him and let him go. I've forgiven him, or at least I've tried to. But I'm not letting him hurt me again. I don't hate him. Hate and anger just spill out onto Trevor, so I'm not holding onto any of that."

She reached out for my hand.

"You need to tell Trevor all of that," her tone had dramatically changed. She was soft. "He told you he'd wait for you. He's not going anywhere. And you need to tell Drew what you just told me. Now, I'm tired. You're welcome to sleep here if you'd like, but I'm going to bed. My boss can be a real monster," she winked at me as she threw the pillow in my direction.

9

I couldn't sleep on Emmie's couch, so I got up before dawn and headed to the shop.

There were a few online orders waiting for me. They were for Jimmy, of course. One order was from my parents, and another was from Beth's mother. Not surprising.

I checked online and found a short obituary. Pettit Funeral Home was handling the pending arrangements.

I could go ahead and start on those two. I was sure there'd be more. I'd told Drew I wanted to check J&M, the company that sent the flowers and made Debbie turn 100 shades of pale. I did a quick web search. There was nothing interesting. The site had a home page and an order page and that was it. There was no information on employees; it was bare bones.

I wasn't going to get anywhere with that. There wouldn't be a huge banner on the website that told me why Debbie acted so strangely when I told her who the flowers were from.

When I didn't know what else to do in my life, I threw myself into the tasks at hand, and that meant putting together the funerary arrangements.

After the previous day, I'd hoped for a quiet one, and my wish was granted for the most part. Around 11, I grabbed some daisies, carnations, roses, and lilies and created a fun and happy arrangement in a white basket.

"That's really pretty, sweetie, but I didn't see anything like that on any of the orders," Emmie stood with her hands on her hips.

"It's not. I thought I'd take it to Trevor."

"Aw. That's sweet."

"Mind if I take a lunch break? I can bring something back for you."

"Where are you going?"

"I'll pick up a sandwich or something. I'm trying to decide. If I was just taking the flowers, I'd walk. Some of the parking lots are only a few blocks away."

"I hear you. Have you ever been over there?"

"Not to Trevor's office. I mean; he's only been there for a few weeks."

The Medical College of Georgia at Augusta University has a rich history in Georgia. It was founded in 1828 and is the state's only public medical school. One of its first buildings still stands at the corner of Telfair and Sixth Streets. Constructed in 1835, the Greek Revival building is used for private events these days, but medical students trained there until 1913.

That structure was renovated in 1989, and to the horror of construction workers, there were layers of human bones and primitive medical tools found in the building's dirt basement.

It was a shallow grave for more than 1,000 bones, the remains of cadavers used to teach medical students.

Dissection of a human body was illegal in Georgia until 1887 unless the body was of an executed criminal, but that didn't stop the doctors. They used some freelance graverobbers and even had one of their own. His name was Grandison Harris, but his nickname was "Resurrection Man." He stole the bodies of the newly buried during the night.

He started out his 50-year career as a graverobber while enslaved by seven doctors at the medical college. After slavery was abolished, Harris became an employee of the school with an official job title of janitor.

Grave robbing was apparently a common practice at the time.

The Medical College of Georgia educates not only physicians but other medical professionals, including dentists and nurses. The campus plus hospital and cancer center covers several blocks. Not only is the medical college and its hospital located there, but there's the Children's Hospital of Georgia, the Charlie Norwood VA Medical Center and University Hospital within the same few blocks. University Hospital was originally known as the city hospital, but it was later renamed University because of its affiliation with the Medical College. University and the medical college parted ways in the 1950s.

Now it was a sprawling complex with not-so-convenient parking to many of the buildings.

I stopped to pick up a couple of subs before I headed to deliver flowers to Trevor.

When I got there, I realized two things – I didn't know which building he was in, and I had no idea where to park. I never delivered flowers to an office. I usually delivered them to patients in the hospitals, so I knew where to park for that.

I found a parking spot a few blocks away, and I gave him a call.

"Good morning, Grace," he said in his soft, calming voice.

"Hi, I wanted to surprise you, but I have no idea where your office is. I have food, but I'm so lost."

He laughed.

"Inside of some of these buildings is super-confusing, too. Just tell me where you are, and I'll come to you."

It took about 15 minutes, but I finally saw him walking toward me.

He smiled as he reached me.

"Sorry, it wasn't much of a surprise."

"Grace, I was surprised with your call. And it's nice to see you," he said taking the flowers and the food from me. "Flowers will be a nice touch to my office. It's pretty dreary in there."

We walked to his building, chatting about the hot weather and his schedule for the day. I followed him through a maze of hallways until we came to his office.

"Even with you leading me here, I don't think I could find it on my own," I said and laughed.

He smiled.

"I know what you mean. It took me a couple of trips down the wrong hallways to figure it out," he said, stopping in front of a door. "And here we are."

He hadn't done much to decorate it, but his degree from the University of Georgia and his medical degree proudly hung on the wall. I put the flowers on his desk, and we sat down to have lunch.

"I'm sorry I didn't get a chance to talk to you last night," I said. "It was a long day, and I fell asleep early. I had a bit of a nap before Drew showed up, and then I went to Emmie's."

He tilted his head and frowned slightly when I mentioned Drew.

"Drew stopped by?" he asked.

"Yeah. Well, I wasn't expecting him, but I had delivered flowers to Peggy and to Jimmy's shop during the day. He wanted to know everyone I'd talked to and what I'd seen.

He nodded slowly.

"Ah. Why Emmie's?" he asked.

"I just needed to be around someone at 10 p.m., and she was the best choice. If she was late for work, I couldn't get upset with her, now could I?" I laughed nervously.

"True."

"How are things going with you?" I queried.

"Busy. I've been trying to prepare for the fall semester, which starts in six weeks. That doesn't seem like enough time," he paused and shook his head. "I've been going over the files of my predecessor to see what information needs to be covered. And there's a lot."

"You look better today than you did at lunch yesterday. You seemed distracted."

"I was on edge. My brothers keep adding to the guest list. They want me to meet people, to network. I guess they still want me to be in a practice. They see this as a temporary position and are still trying to push me to be like them. But I don't want to talk about my brothers. A beautiful woman brought me flowers and lunch."

"It's not much, but you got lunch yesterday. It's my turn."

"I'm glad for lunch. You know I have that meeting tonight, right? I'm on the board of the clinic where I used to work."

"Oh yeah. I remember you told me that. You seemed to enjoy being there."

"I did," he said and shifted the subject. "How has your day gone? Any more visits from Drew?"

"Not today, but there are orders coming in for me to take to the funeral home later."

"I thought Jazzy or Emmie did the deliveries?"

"Most of the time, but I thought I'd to it tonight."

He looked down at his food. Like everyone else, Trevor didn't like my contact with Drew. I wasn't going to back down, and I wasn't going to stop. I couldn't understand why everyone was upset about it. From there, the conversation focused on the weddings I had coming up over the weekend. We also talked about his mother's flower garden.

"Thank you for the flowers. They brighten up the place," he said as I started to leave.

"That's why I do what I do. I love flowers."

"Mama would've loved this arrangement," he said wistfully.

"I thought of her and her love for lilies when I put those in there."

He smiled.

"Thank you. That means a lot to me. I'll walk you out of here, so you don't get lost. It's definitely a maze."

The rest of the day seemed to drag along, as Emmie and I worked on several more arrangements for Jimmy's funeral.

"Emmie, I'm going to run these to the funeral home, and

then I'll probably head home. Could you close up shop again for me?" I asked.

She tilted her head at me.

"Of course. You never make deliveries. And this makes three in two days? Are you sure you want to?"

I didn't answer right away. Emmie folded her arms against her chest.

"Spying for Drew?"

"These flowers aren't going to deliver themselves."

"Yes, but I could do that for you, Grace, so I know there's an ulterior motive."

"Oh stop, Emmie. It's not spying, and you know you're just as curious. You're just jealous."

"Always," she admitted, grinning broadly. "Such a mess. Too many suspects"

I raised an eyebrow at her.

"Suspects? Really? Weren't you just fussing at me for helping with this case? What's your involvement? Is there a suspect board hiding in your room somewhere that I couldn't see?" I teased her.

"No, sweetie, but we should really do that," she grinned mischievously before becoming serious again. "It's getting hard to keep track of them all. I never knew so many people had reasons to want to kill Jimmy."

"Sadly, that's true. I always liked him, and I thought other people did, too."

"You'd better tell me if you find out anything. I'm interested to see who all shows up for his visitation and funeral."

"That's one of the reasons I want to deliver these flowers. I want some details on when all that is taking place."

Emmie helped me load the van, and I drove to Pettit Funeral Home. The delivery entrance was in the back. I saw Nancy Pettit as soon as I opened the back door. Her family had owned and run the place for generations.

"Well, hello there, Grace. It's been a long time since I've seen you delivering flowers," she said. Nancy was in her 40s, thin with jet-black hair and always dressed in a suit.

"I know. This one is personal. Jimmy was a friend of the family, and he was one of my best customers. I will miss him a lot," I replied. "And I have several to bring in."

"How's Jazzy? I haven't seen her in a while."

"Oh, she's fine. She has been going to Augusta Tech getting a medical assistant certificate. She's got a job during the week working in a doctor's office to see if this is what she wants to do. She works Friday evenings and Saturdays helping with weddings right now."

"Not that I don't like seeing you, but I've missed Jazzy."

"You aren't the only one. I'm thinking she'll be back. She told me several months ago that she wasn't sure she wanted to do anything in medicine."

"Oh?"

"I think she'd really like to do cosmetology or wedding planning or something like that."

"Who's she working with?"

"Beth's husband and Trevor's brother."

"Ah. I'd heard you were seeing Trevor Blake."

I smiled.

"We're good friends right now."

Nancy simply nodded and led me to the room where the body would be placed for the viewing. The room was empty except for a couple of chairs and a table. There was an open space for the casket.

"They're still preparing him," she said.

I nodded.

"Thanks. I don't want to know anything else," I said.

Nancy chuckled.

"I completely understand."

"How is the family holding up?" I asked.

"About as well as can be expected, I suppose. Jake came in and made all the arrangements," she said. "It's been very strange, though.

Peggy kept calling while he was here and making him change things. I don't know why she just didn't come herself. It made it hard on him. He was frustrated with the whole process."

"I saw Peggy yesterday morning. I can understand her wanting their son to do it. Becca didn't come with him?"

"No just Jake."

"Nancy, I was wondering when the funeral and visitation would be. I didn't see anything online yet."

"They are only doing a graveside service," she said. "Visitation will be Friday night, and then after the funeral at the graveside Saturday."

I placed a wreath in the room.

"I've got several more. I'm parked out back."

"That's fine. Just put them in the room, and I'll arrange them later."

I walked back to the van to get another flower, and when I returned, I could hear shouting.

"I don't care. I want to see my husband now."

It was Peggy Hughes, and her voice was shrill. I couldn't hear the response probably because Nancy was professional and wouldn't raise her voice.

"Where is he?" she shrieked.

The sound traveled down a corridor. I ducked into another one of the rooms so she couldn't see or hear me.

"Mama, calm down," Jake sounded close.

The room I was in wasn't being used, and the lights were off. I pulled into a corner. They sounded as though they were on the other side of the wall in the corridor.

"Calm down? You want me to calm down? Your father is dead, and it's all your fault. If you hadn't squandered your money in Vegas, your father wouldn't have been forced to have that meeting the other night. He wouldn't be dead. He wouldn't have been killed."

The hair on the back of my neck stood on end and a chill ran down my spine as she said that. Who was she talking about, and was that what scared Jimmy so much?

"Me? You're blaming this on me? How can you say that when you've been running around behind his back with a man who wants Dad's businesses - and your other assets."

The sound of a slap jolted me. I assumed it was Peggy hitting Jake.

"Don't you ever talk to your mama like that again."

That statement confirmed it. There was a pause and then I heard a third voice.

"What are the two of you doing?" Becca sounded exasperated.

"What are you doing here?" Peggy asked.

"Jake told me you were coming. I figured you'd try to make a scene, so I dropped everything to come over here. What's wrong with the two of you?"

There was a pause. Then Becca continued.

"You both should be breathing a sigh of relief. Mama, you and Daddy have been fighting all my life. You should enjoy the peace. And Jake, you can try to stop being like him to please him. The man was no good. I, for one, am glad he's gone. Now stop it. Both of you, just stop."

"Don't say things like that, Becca. Your father was a good man."

"My father and your husband were two completely different people. You might've been able to put up with him, but I couldn't. Nothing I ever did made him happy. And look what he's done to Jake."

I stood in the corner and waited for someone to say something else, but after several moments, I heard nothing. I was almost afraid to come out of my hiding place. I waited until I was sure there was no one outside the room, and I peeked around the corner. The hallway was empty. I took the flowers into the appropriate room and brought the rest of them in without seeing anyone. I'd always thought it was creepy to be in a funeral home alone during the day. I took a breath and started to head out the door when I saw

Nancy. I was glad to see her.

"I guess you overheard the ruckus," she said.

"Couldn't not hear it," I answered.

She laughed.

"Fortunately, they weren't loud enough to raise the dead."

I chuckled and nervously looked around.

"Are you sure? It was a little creepy in here after the noise settled."

"Yes. Everyone is where they are supposed to be," she said in that monotone voice reserved especially for undertakers. "Now, you see what I mean by the Hughes family being difficult."

"Yeah. I'm finding out a lot about them. Things weren't what I thought they were."

"They never are, Grace. They never are. But from the looks of the room, people cared about Jimmy Hughes," she said.

"Yes, they did. I'll probably see you again," I said as I headed to the door.

When I got into the delivery van, I sat there for a few minutes. I knew I needed to call Drew. I wanted to know more about Jimmy's meeting to cover Jake's gambling debts. Was that what Jimmy was so afraid of when he met with me? I wanted to cry. He seemed to love Peggy so much.

I stared at my phone before sending a text to Emmie telling her I was finished, but I still needed her to close up shop. I didn't need Drew showing up at my doorstep again, so I bit the bullet and called him.

"Hello, Grace," he said.

"Hi. I'm getting ready to leave the funeral home."

"Ah. You must have something for me."

"I do. I delivered some flowers for Jimmy's funeral and visitation. I went out the back to bring in an arrangement and Peggy and Jake must've come in through the front doors. They were arguing, but they didn't see me. I hid in one of the other rooms."

"Okay. What were they arguing about?"

"Both of them blamed the other for Jimmy's death, but apparently, Jimmy was meeting with someone to cover Jake's gambling debts. She told Jake that it was his fault Jimmy was dead. Then Jake said it was her fault because she was seeing someone who wanted to take over their businesses."

"Ah."

"Then Becca came in to break up the fight. She told them they should breathe a sigh of relief because there wouldn't be any more between Peggy and Jimmy and Jake didn't have to try to please his father."

"Ouch. That was cold."

"I knew Jimmy had issues, but I didn't realize just how dysfunctional they all were."

"No kidding."

"I don't know if that helps you or not, but I think there's a lot of stuff we just don't know."

"I can promise you you're right about that, Grace. And it does help. It tells me that Peggy has been lying to me about a few things."

"You won't tell her that I told you that, will you?"

"No, Grace, I won't, but it helps me to ask some more detailed questions the next time I talk to her. When's the funeral home visitation?"

"Friday night. Funeral is at 1 p.m. Saturday. Why on God's green earth anyone would have an outdoor funeral at midday in June in Augusta is beyond me. But that's when it is."

"I take it you'll be at both places."

"Yes, I will, and if there are more flowers, I'll be back at the funeral home. She wanted to see his body, but it wasn't ready yet. Drew, was it bad?"

He didn't answer right away.

"Define bad. I mean he was shot in the back of the head."

I paused as an image started to flash in my mind.

"Never mind. You don't have to say another word."

"Good, Grace. You really don't want to know the answer to

that."

"I think you just put an image in my head I can't unsee."

He laughed.

"Try not to think about it, okay?"

"I'll try, Drew. I can't make any promises."

"I appreciate your help."

"Drew, will I have to wait to hear about an arrest from the radio or newspaper?"

He paused.

"I'll see what I can do. I can't make any promises on that," he said.

"I understand."

"No, you don't," he said playfully.

"You're probably right."

"Listen Grace. Thanks for your help. If I find out anything, I'll let you know. Have a good night."

"You, too," I said as I ended the call. I breathed a sigh of relief because he didn't ask me what I was doing the rest of the evening. I figured he'd be following up on my lead.

After I left the funeral home, I decided to stop by Trevor's and work on his mother's rose garden. I'd added several new flower beds that needed minor weeding. Weeds grew so fast in the summer. I'd also planted a small vegetable garden. There would likely be tomatoes and peppers that needed harvesting. Despite the fact that his home was in the middle of town, he had a large lot. It wasn't a flat backyard, either. The house was on an incline, and there were different levels to the back yard. On one level was a patio and pool, and on the lowest level, there was a flat lush lawn and Miss Harper's rose garden. When his parents were alive, the rose garden was their social hub with many parties held in the space.

He wasn't at home when I got there, but I knew he wouldn't be. The neighbors knew me by now, so they didn't question my appearance in the yard. A lot of times, his neighbor on the left waved at me. Mr. Johnson was a widower who I think was lonely. He'd sometimes ask me gardening questions, but he often just wanted to linger in the garden to see its progress and have some company. Trevor had a small pool house that I used to change my clothes. I put my ear buds in and cranked up the music. This was as much therapy to me as sitting and talking to a counselor.

As I worked in his yard, I could imagine so many improvements I'd make, but it wasn't my yard. I was just thankful to touch the dirt since I didn't have any of my own. Any suggestion I made was fine with Trevor, and I was loving how it turned out. The yard had beautiful gardenias, hydrangeas, and camellias, all of which needed some tender loving care. I'd added some extra flower beds with petunias, pansies, and impatiens. I wanted the yard to have something in bloom all year if possible.

I'd applied my mosquito repellent, so I didn't get eaten up while working in the yard. Eventually, I just lost track of time as I listened to music and worked the soil.

At one point, I looked up to see a water bottle being dangled in front of me.

I took my earbuds out as Trevor knelt down in front of me.

"Hi. I thought you had to go to a board meeting," I said.

He smiled and shook his head.

"Do you have any idea what time it is?"

"No, I got lost in the music."

He laughed.

"Obviously, because it's nearly 9."

"That late already?"

"Yeah. That late."

I stood up and took the water bottle from him.

"Thank you."

He turned his head to look at the area.

"I love what you've done down here," he said, looking back at me. "I remember how the garden used to look when Mama was alive and able to tend to it. She loved having her garden club over. There were so many different varieties of flowers."

"They're still here. They just need a little help to come back."

"So, what else would you like to do to this area?" he asked casually resting his hands on his hips and gazing over the space.

"There are so many things I'd love to do out here. You could have a covered deck right over there," I said and pointed to a tree-fringed corner of the yard. "It would be a great spot to sit at on evenings after you get home, and you could have guests over there. You could decorate it with hanging white lights. There is room for a firepit, which would be great in the fall. It would be so pretty."

He smiled.

"What?"

"I haven't seen you excited about anything except my yard in a long time," he chuckled. "I'm not really sure how to take that."

"It's such a beautiful space. I love being out here."

"I can tell, but the humidity is still 100 percent. Don't you want to go inside?"

"The outdoors brings me peace."

"Ah, bad afternoon?"

"It was disconcerting, yes," I said.

He began walking and motioned for me to follow.

"Hang on. I picked some of the vegetables from the garden," I said as I detoured to the vegetable garden and picked up the basket with the tomatoes, cucumbers, bell peppers, and yellow squash.

I brought it over to him.

"I don't need to go inside, Trevor. I must smell awful. I should go home and take a shower and go to bed."

He stopped and laughed.

"I worked in an ER. You don't know how bad some things can smell," he said.

I wrinkled my nose.

"Okay, but only for a few minutes."

"That's fine. I want to hear about your horrible day."

I laughed.

"Are you sure about that? Why don't you tell me about your

day instead?"

"Things are getting better. I'm looking forward to interacting with the students," he said. "And some beautiful flowers brightened up my office."

I smiled.

"I'm glad to hear that."

When I stepped into his house, I felt like I was walking into a freezer as the controlled air hit my sweat-covered skin and damp hair. I opened the bottle and guzzled it.

"Are you all right?" he asked.

"Yeah, I guess I stayed out longer than I should have."

"Want a snack?" he asked, making a bee line for the kitchen.

"Depends on the snack. My mother should be pulling out her lemon pound cake recipe about now. I'd love some of that," I said and laughed.

"The ultimate comfort food," he replied.

"Something like that. I went to the funeral home to deliver flowers, and Peggy showed up demanding to see Jimmy."

"Okay?"

"Yeah, they were still preparing the body so they told her she couldn't. She got irate. About that time, Jake showed up. She got into a yelling match with him. They wound up both accusing each other of killing Jimmy. Then, Peggy slapped Jake for good measure before Becca came and broke it up."

Trevor furrowed his brow and started to say something then shook his head.

"I know. I was confused, too. Jake said it was her affair with Steve, and Peggy said it was Jake's gambling. That's what they blamed the other for."

"Jake has a gambling problem, too?" Trevor raised an eyebrow.

"Like father, like son, I guess."

"Where were you when all of this happened?"

"I was hiding in one of the other rooms."

He laughed and opened the stainless-steel refrigerator. He

stood there for a few minutes to allow the cool air to wash over him.

"It wasn't this hot yesterday when we had our picnic," he said.

"No, it was surprisingly nice for 90 degrees, but the weather here can change in the blink of an eye," I laughed.

"North Carolina can be much cooler than here, especially near the mountains and even in the summer," he said. "One thing I didn't miss about Augusta was the heat and the humidity."

He pulled a plastic container out of the refrigerator and placed it on the counter. Inside it was some juicy red watermelon he'd cut into cubes. I took one of the pieces and savored it.

"Oh, wow. This tastes so good," I said.

"I take it you haven't eaten anything else besides lunch today?"

"No, but this is better than anything I could've picked up for dinner anyway."

"What are your plans for tomorrow?"

"I don't have any yet."

"Did you call Drew yet?" he tilted his head.

"I called him when I left the funeral home. I've seen Drew enough over the past couple of days."

He raised an eyebrow.

"Ah now the real reason I found you in my yard tonight."

"Yes and no. I hadn't been over in a few days, and there were some things that needed to be tended. You can see the harvest. I could make some awesome salsa with what I picked tonight," I said with a smile.

"Salsa with dinner tomorrow or Friday night?" he asked.

"Yes, we could do that."

He took one of the watermelon cubes out of the container and casually asked the next question.

"So why were you hiding from Drew?"

I glanced around and picked up another watermelon cube.

"I was right," he said as he ate the watermelon.

"This time last year Drew and I were in a honeymoon phase.

He wasn't drinking; he was going to counseling, but then around the Fourth of July everything fell apart. He started drinking again because he kept blaming himself for Mark shooting Linda then himself. Everything in our world came crashing down. Drew's acting the same way he did last June. He showed up at my apartment twice yesterday. I think he wanted to ask me out."

I watched Trevor's face as I said that. I couldn't decipher his expression. Was that fear that I saw when I said that? He quickly recovered and put on his doctor face. There was no expression.

"How do you feel about it?" he asked in the most clinical tone.

"You sound like my therapist, Dr. Blake."

He leaned on the kitchen island and stared at me.

"Well, since you haven't been going to the therapist…"

"I've been some, and I'm working on the things she said to. I've had a few major breakthroughs. I realize that Drew's drinking wasn't the only problem in our marriage."

He tilted his head.

"So how do you feel about his current behavior?"

I wanted to leave, but that was one of my problems. I avoided things instead of dealing with them. I tried not to talk about things, changed the subject. That was good in its way, but it was also bad. And Trevor wasn't backing down, either.

I leaned on the island, too; my face was close to his.

"It's unsettling. It scares me. I don't want to go back into a relationship with Drew. I can't take the rollercoaster any longer. If he would've stayed with me in the fall instead of going through with the divorce, I would've worked things out. But he didn't; he left," I took a deep breath. "And I have come a long way in a few months. Thanks to people who care about me. I've gained confidence in myself. I've healed some. I don't walk on eggshells anymore. I'm not worried about making anyone angry."

I smiled at him and straightened up.

"And I'm not going back. I'm not going back to Drew, and

I'm not going back to living in that environment."

Trevor smiled. He looked relieved.

"I'm glad to hear it," he said.

Then he tilted his head and laughed.

"What?"

"You have a cute smudge of dirt right there," he said, touching my cheek.

"Did you get it?" I asked.

"No. I think I'll leave it there. You look like you're getting ready to slide into second base or something."

"Thanks. I think."

"When was the last time you checked your phone?"

"I guess when I called Drew, then texted Emmie that I was done for the day. I dropped the van off and picked up my car and came here."

"Well, I've got texts from Emmie, Beth, and your mom checking on you."

"Oh, sorry."

I pulled out my phone and checked for messages. Yep, they were there.

"Why do you need to get a dress from Beth?"

"I need something appropriate for Saturday night."

"I'd love to buy you a dress for that."

"Trevor, that's sweet of you, and we've been through this so many times. I am a big girl. I can take care of myself. I appreciate the offer, though."

His face fell.

"Besides, Trevor, Beth thinks I'm an adult-size Barbie. She doesn't have girls, so she has no one to play dress-up with but me."

He laughed.

"And she probably has just the thing in her closet without me trying to go out and buy something. There's no need for me to reinvent the wheel," I smiled at him and grabbed one last piece of watermelon. "Thank you for the watermelon and the bottle of water.

I need to go. I'm really tired, and I'm a dirty mess."

"All right. I'll let you go this time," he said playfully.

10

I tossed and turned most of the night. I did fall asleep long enough to have a dream, and it was one of those dreams that connected several dots.

I was back in my shop and making the arrangement Jimmy wanted to take to Peggy.

"Shug, I need to use your restroom," Jimmy said.

"No worries. You know where it is, and if you want to relax in my office while I do this, you're more than welcome."

"I may just do that. I've been on my feet all day."

What I saw in my dream that I didn't see in reality was what happened next. I saw Jimmy go into my office and pull the tape out of my desk. He took the folder he had in his hands and crawled under the desk, taping the folder to the bottom of it. He checked it several times to make sure it was secure. Then he sat down to wait for me to finish.

I woke up immediately after the dream. I replayed the events of that night in my head.

It's true that Jimmy sat in my office while I made the arrangement. It was also true that I couldn't remember seeing that folder in his hands when he left my shop. I handed him the cut-crystal vase, and that was all he was holding.

I jumped out of bed and dressed quickly. I could put my makeup on and brush my teeth at the shop. I needed to see if what I dreamed was reality and what was in that folder that he'd so nervously clutched while he was in my office. I drove as fast as was legally possible and maybe a little faster. Once I parked, I rushed to get inside the shop to my desk. I dropped to my knees, crawling under my desk and twisting to look up. I wasn't sure why I was surprised to see a manila folder taped to my desk drawer. I reached up, tearing it from its fasteners. Sitting on the floor, I gazed at the envelope. My hands shook as I opened the folder. There were emails, invoices, and what looked to be copies of pages from a ledger. I moved to my chair, glancing at the clock on the wall. It wasn't quite 7. I thumbed through the papers again.

I pulled out an email from J&M. This didn't give me any more information about the company than what I'd seen on its website. The email address was simply "office manager" at the J&M site. It wasn't signed, but it instructed someone at Jimmy's shop to create bogus invoices. There were several similar emails. I wasn't sure what that meant. Could it have been money laundering? I wasn't sure. I flipped through the other pages. There was another ledger and pages of photocopies of checks made out to Debbie and signed by Debbie. There were several checks to a page. They went back at least five years. I was sure that was enough to buy her swanky house on the river. I wondered if this was what Debbie had been looking for the day after Jimmy's murder. There were other pieces of financial information in the folder.

This was definitely something Drew needed to see. I wondered why Jimmy had left the folder in my office. There wasn't any kind of note included. I was sure he didn't mean for me to see any of it. Had he planned on coming back to get it?

"Oh, Jimmy. What were you involved in?"

I stopped flipping through the pages and stared at my phone. I'd seen Drew more in the past several hours than I'd wanted. But this was information that I couldn't hold onto. While I hesitated in calling him, I snapped several photos of the information. I could look over it later. And to be on the safe side, I emailed the photos to myself, deleting them from my phone once I found they'd arrived in my email. I had a feeling Drew would ask to see my phone. This way I didn't have to lie completely if he asked if I had photos.

"Good morning. I didn't expect to hear from you so early in the day," he said as he answered.

"Hi. I have some information for you at my office. It's pretty important."

"I'll be there in 10," he said.

I stared at the orders. I needed to work, but I didn't want to start anything and get interrupted by Drew.

It didn't take him 10 minutes to get to my shop. It was more like five. I heard him knocking.

"You're an early bird this morning," he said as he came in. He handed me a paper cup and a paper bag.

"Couldn't sleep," I answered. "What's this?"

"Breakfast. Knowing you, you haven't had anything."

I tilted my head. Had he been on the way to see me when I called him? I took a sip of the sweet tea; it tasted good on the hot summer morning. It might not have been 7 a.m. yet, but the humidity was already high.

"So good. Thank you," I answered, walking into my office. He followed me and sat in the chair across from me. I glanced at the folders on my desk.

"Eat," he said as he pulled something out of his bag. It looked like a breakfast biscuit. I took the wrapped item out of my bag. It was a chicken biscuit. "I promise not to tell the doc I gave you that for breakfast."

I laughed.

"That's a good idea. How much do I owe you?"

He narrowed his eyes at me and shook his head "no."

"Nothing. Don't even go there," he said as he took a bite of his biscuit. "So, why couldn't you sleep? Bad dream you called to tell me about?"

"No actually. It wasn't bad. It was one of those dreams that

Trevor told you was me connecting the dots; except that my brain tends to add in details when it connects dots."

He tilted his head at me.

"How so?"

I took a bite out of the biscuit and pushed the folder to him.

"Remember when I said that Jimmy had a folder when he came here, and that I didn't see the folder when I described your crime scene?"

"Yeah. There was no folder at the crime scene," he said as he picked it up and started to thumb through the pages.

"He had me create a flower arrangement for Peggy, and while I did that, he waited in my office. But later, when I gave him the vase, he didn't have anything in his hands. It didn't occur to me at the time. So, this morning, I dreamt that I saw him in my office, taping the folder underneath my desk."

He didn't look at me while I talked; the contents of the folder had his full attention. He only glanced at me when I paused.

"And was the folder where you saw it in your dream?"

"Yeah. It was taped under there with lots of tape. It's pretty heavy. I don't think he wanted it going anywhere."

Drew sucked in a deep breath.

"Grace, this is a goldmine."

"I wonder if some of that is what Debbie was looking for when I stopped by with the flowers."

He stared at me.

"You looked through these, didn't you?"

I smiled.

"Of course, I did. I didn't know if I needed to call you or Peggy to come pick it up."

"Uh-huh, Grace. A likely story."

"Definitely incriminates Debbie."

"It looks like something for further investigation," he responded. His poker face was ever perfect, and his tone was deadpan.

"What do you make of those other emails from J&M?" I

attempted to push him into telling me something. I know what I made of them, but I wanted to know if I was right. He glanced up at me and closed the folder.

"I could speculate a lot of things just by glancing at these papers, but I won't know what it means until I take a deeper look."

"I guess I won't know what that deeper look means."

"It could mean a lot of things, Grace. It could mean nothing. It's just paper until I can do some digging on it. I can speculate anything."

I let out an exasperated sigh. I wanted answers. I wanted to know what Jimmy was involved in. I wanted to know what was up with Debbie and what she was looking for when I interrupted her. I wanted to know who could've killed Jimmy and why. I also wondered why he left those papers with me.

"So, speculate, Drew. Tell me what you think is going on."

He smiled.

"My guesses aren't what will put someone behind bars," he said. "But I have been following up on your hunch about J&M."

"I couldn't find anything, and I wasn't sure where else to look."

"I have access to resources you don't. J&M looks perfect on paper, but it's a little too perfect."

"That's interesting."

"Yeah, that's what I thought, too. It looks like it could be a shell company, and I need to see what these emails about invoices are. It could mean that Jimmy or Jimmy's business was laundering money for someone. Debbie is super suspicious, and she could be arrested on something very soon."

My mouth dropped. Not because I was surprised that Debbie was going to be arrested, but I was surprised that Drew told me this tidbit.

"What do you mean?"

"We can't prove a murder. We do have evidence of embezzlement, and those checks make a greater case for that. And these emails. The name on them is Jimmy's, but I'm not 100 percent certain it was him. That's what needs to be researched. It could've been him or the email return address could've been faked. People fake emails all the time. Debbie could've been the one doing the laundering. I don't know that yet."

"Wow."

"I know. Give me a few more days, and I'll know more. I'm waiting to see if she slips up. The conversations you've overheard have given me a lot of info to go on So, consider breakfast as a tiny way of saying thanks."

"No problem. I guess that folder will keep you busy for a while."

He chuckled.

"Always putting me to work," he said. His smile quickly vanished as though a thought had interrupted him. "Did he leave you anything else?"

Before I could answer, Drew stood up and gestured toward my desk. I moved out of the way as he crawled under it.

"I thought I got everything from there," I said as I watched him.

"You did," he said as he popped out from underneath the desk. "Do you mind if I look in the drawers?"

"Go ahead."

I hadn't opened my desk drawers since Jimmy had been in there. I hadn't been in my office since that night. Jimmy had been the last person to sit in that other chair. I watched as Drew rummaged through them. He found the usual things in my desk – pens, paperclips, a stapler, a candy bar, and a tube of lipstick. But when he came to any other clues, he came up empty.

"Thanks, Grace," he said. "I should head on now."

"Of course. Thanks for breakfast."

"Don't mention it," he said as he walked out of my shop.

By the time Emmie showed up for work, I'd already finished several funeral sprays. I was running out of room in the work area.

"Wow. Someone has been busy today," she said.

"I got here early."

"Uh huh. What's going on, sweetie?"

"Oh, those dreams again."

"Tell me more," she said as she put her purse down and leaned onto the worktable.

"Jimmy left me some clues," I said as I picked up my phone and opened my email to show her the photos.

Emmie perked up.

"Clues?"

"Yeah, he taped a folder under my desk. It was packed full of papers," I said as I moved closer to her to show her the photographs. "I should print them out. This will be too tiny to see on the screen."

I showed her my phone. Her eyes widened and her mouth dropped as she enlarged a few of the photos.

"I told you that Debbie was up to no good. Did you add up these checks?" she asked me.

"No, I haven't had much time. I flipped through the pages and called Drew. He was here for a while, The plot thickens. I wonder what all this means."

"What did Drew say?"

I cleared my throat.

"Grace, I can't speculate. There's too much here for me to investigate," I attempted my best Drew impression, causing Emmie to laugh.

"You do a very good Drew," she said.

"You think?"

"What's wrong, sweetie?"

"He brought me breakfast."

Emmie shook her head in disapproval.

"You need to tell him how you feel and soon," she said softly.

"I know. It wasn't the time this morning, though. I had all that info from Jimmy. He needed to see it, and I didn't want to muddy the waters with talk about us."

I walked back to the funeral spray I was working on.

"Listen, Emmie. I need to go to Beth's later and find a dress for this weekend. I'll probably do that toward the end of the day."

"Fine, but are you sure Drew didn't say anything else?"

"He said it was just paper until he could investigate. I mean it definitely looks like Debbie was stealing money. And those emails make it look like someone was laundering money. I wonder about this J&M group. It sounds like they were pretty shady."

"True. Is he going to update you?'

"This is my ex we're talking about, Emmie. Since when has Drew wanted to share information willingly with me?"

"I know it is, sweetie, but you've given him a ton of information."

"So, he should reward me for that? Is that what you're saying?" I laughed at the thought.

"Possibly, but I hope he'll keep you in the loop."

"Me, too, in a way. If I can limit my contact with him, all the better."

"Whatever you say. Tell me what I need to do before you go."

"There are several orders for Jimmy's funeral. Most of them are from people we know. Nothing unusual. And I almost forgot about the Signers Monument ceremony on July 4. We will have a couple of wreaths for that," I said. "I need some red, white, and blue flowers for those."

Emmie laughed.

"How could you forget about that?"

"July 4 was a rough day last year," I said. "But I did learn a few things about Augusta's history last year."

"You were telling me about that. How cool is it that two of Georgia's three signers of the Declaration of Independence are buried in the middle of the street in downtown?" she asked, her voice brimming with sarcasm.

"It is cool, Emmie. You know I love history, and Augusta has some great history. Not long after I went to that ceremony, I found one of the history videos the newspaper has created. It was really interesting."

Emmie rolled her eyes at me, so I stuck my tongue out at her.

The Signers Monument was in the middle of the street. Actually, it was sort of a median on Greene Street. When it was dedicated in 1848, it was more on the lawn of the old courthouse and city hall, which was built in the 1820s. It was a beautiful building with a dome and a clock on its face and a statue at the peak of the dome. It was demolished in the 1950s for the current Municipal Building, or the "Marble Palace," as it was irreverently nicknamed by a columnist from the newspaper in the 1960s. The statue of Lady Justice, which remained after the demolition, doesn't have a blindfold, which goes to show that justice hasn't always been blind in the city. Crony politics ran rampant for years and inspired a novel and movie called "Col. Effingham's Raid," a thinly veiled look at politics in Richmond County and Augusta in the early 20th century. Rumors swirled for decades about the discovery of a still on the roof of the courthouse. Whether people were making moonshine, or it was just a remnant of a raid no one will ever know.

The Signers Monument is a 50-foot tall obelisk in honor of Georgia's three signers of the Declaration of Independence. Augusta was the state capital at one time, and one of the signers of the document had lived in Augusta. George Walton, whose Meadow Garden home is now a museum, was a colonel during the American Revolution and served as the state's governor for two terms.

The two other signers weren't from Augusta. They were Lyman Hall and Button Gwinnett. Hall was a physician who later served as governor and a judge. He died in Burke County, which is adjacent to Augusta's Richmond County line to the south. Gwinnett was born in England and moved to Georgia. He was a trader and was elected to the Georgia Assembly. He also served for a brief time as governor.

Beneath the stone obelisk is a crypt containing the remains of Hall and Walton. No one knows exactly where Gwinnett is buried.

He was killed during a duel against a longtime political rival in Savannah in 1777. He is believed to have been buried in Savannah's Colonial Park Cemetery.

The July 4 ceremony was started by an Augusta-born lawyer who visits his mother on his birthday each year. Of course, his birthday is July 4. He thought it was odd that Augusta had such a great tie to the nation's founding, yet it went unobserved. Members from groups such as the Daughters of the American Revolution and Sons of the American Revolution place wreaths at the monument during the ceremony.

Since I'd made a few of those wreaths for it and the ceremony was held in the early morning of Independence Day, I'd decided I wanted to go last year. Things had been going well with Drew at that point. He'd been going to counseling, and we'd just gotten back from an incredibly romantic week at Beth and Knox's house at Edisto Beach, South Carolina. I thought things were going to work out for us.

But Independence Day brought with it a flurry of memories related to his friends, Mark and Linda. We used to spend that holiday with them.

He didn't want to go to the ceremony with me, so I left him at home. My parents had a cookout, and I went there next – without Drew. And Emmie asked me to go with her and the boys to see the fireworks. I did all of it without Drew. When I got home, I found him passed out on the couch with an empty bottle of whiskey, and my heart broke. He stopped going to counseling not long after that, and our marriage declined rapidly.

I looked at Emmie.

"I'm sorry, Grace. You never told me what happened that day. You said that's when he started drinking again, but you kept it inside for months."

"I know, Emmie. Apparently, I'm good at that. But this July 4 should be much better."

"Do you have plans?"

"Not yet. My parents will be cooking out, so if nothing else, I'll go over there with Zack, Sarah, and the kids."

"I don't have the boys this year, but I know how much you love the fireworks. We can go together, sweetie," she said and smiled.

"We've still got two weeks to think about it."

"True. But if you and Trevor don't want a third wheel, I completely understand."

I laughed.

"I'll let you know. We need to figure out what flowers I'll need for those July 4th wreaths. We'll need some blue ones, so they are patriotic and all that. I'd like to try something different, so I'll leave it up to you"

"That sounds good," she said.

"We've got a lot of arrangements to get done. We'll need to take another trip to the funeral home before 4, and I'll probably go to Beth's after that."

Around 3, I loaded the van and dropped off the flowers. It was peaceful with no shouting family members. I returned the delivery van to my shop and peeked in to check on Emmie.

"I'm going to Beth's," I said.

"Have fun with that, sweetie."

"Of course. I love dressing up in her clothes. She has great taste."

Emmie wrinkled her nose, and I laughed.

"Emmie, when it comes to classics with a hint of sexy, she has impeccable taste, and you know it."

"True, but I don't like the classics. Give me bohemian styles any day of the week."

"And that fits your personality. Sometimes, I look more homeless than boho."   I was somewhere in the middle of the two of them. I liked elements of both and sometimes wore the contrasting styles at the same time.

"Well, you and I both know that I have to look elegant and classic Saturday night for Trevor."

"I know, sweetie. I know."

"Thank you for switching your weekends so you could cover for me with the weddings we have."

"Grace, this is a big deal for you, and we both know it. You and I are best friends," she walked over and gave me a sisterly hug.

"I couldn't do any of this without you and Beth, and I really miss Jazzy. The place just isn't the same without her."

"True, but at least she's here on Saturdays. That makes at least one day of the week a little brighter."

11

I had texted Beth to let her know I was on the way, so she was expecting me.

Beth lived a few blocks from Trevor in a beautiful older home in the Summerville area. One of the things I loved about that section of town was the architectural variety. The homes had influences from neoclassical to Italianate to Queen Anne. They weren't cookie cutter in the least. They had an abundance of character and charm. And Beth's home was exactly what I'd expect from her. It was Tudor style with its slanted, gabled roof and the exposed exterior wooden beams. Inside, there were pointed archways instead of doors, balancing the darkness and light in the home. The ceilings had dark exposed wood, and the formal spaces featured dark wood paneling. The other parts of the home were lighter and expressed more of Beth's personal style. The home was perfect for Beth who was a series of contrasts. Like Beth, the house had its stiff formal facades, but in the family spaces, it was warm and welcoming.

"I thought I was going to have to bring dresses to the shop and have you try them on there," she said with her hands on her hips as she greeted me at the door.

"I told you I'd come by, and here I am."

She rolled her eyes at me.

"It's really not going to be as bad as you're making it. I promise."

We walked up the wooden staircase to the master suite. The

room was massive. It was painted white so she could showcase the artwork she'd collected over the years. Beth's bedroom was her sanctuary. She liked to support local artists, and there were plenty of them to keep her busy. Her walk-in closet was huge, nearly half the size of my apartment. She had a gorgeous, cherry sleigh bed covered in white linens. The room would've felt bare except for all of the beautiful art on the wall. The colors were rich, and the subjects were varied.

I recognized one of Emmie's pieces immediately. Emmie liked to paint abstract, geometric designs. She used bold strokes and bright paints. Her artwork reflected her personality.

"I like that one," I pointed to Emmie's piece.

"Yes, that was from her first art exhibition that you held at your shop. I bought it on the spot, and it fits in nicely," Beth said.

"I remember that. We probably need to do another one, maybe closer to September. We could have some tables set up outside the shop on the grass and have hors d'oeuvres, too."

"Ooh, I like that idea. Sounds like a fun party," she said with a big smile.

"That one will probably be fun. This one not so much."

"Don't look at it that way, Grace. It can be fun. You'll be with me. I promise you'll have a good time."

"I appreciate your positive attitude."

"Come look at these," she said as she stood next to her bed. She had three dresses lying across the bed. Two were black, but one was magenta. She knew I loved shades of pinks, wines, and purples. I was drawn to that one. She followed my gaze and picked the magenta one up.

"This one?" she asked with a grin.

"It's pretty, but would it be okay for Saturday?"

"Why not?"

"It's not black."

She laughed.

"It's summer. The guys can wear black. It will be okay. I

promise," she said.

"What are you wearing?"

"I have a royal blue dress I want to wear. It's summer, so I'm going with light and festive," she said and smiled.

I tried on the pink dress. It came to just above my knees. The sleeveless dress was made of chiffon. It was light, and the skirt had a lot of movement to it. There was an attractive ruching around the waist.

"Okay, I'll borrow this one," I said as I spun around to watch the skirt flounce.

There was no need to drag things out. She scowled at me.

"You don't want to at least try the other two?" she asked as I changed back into my clothes.

"Why should I? You just pulled the other two out for show. You knew I'd want to wear this one to begin with."

"Well, that's true."

I laughed.

"So, what's the real reason you wanted me to come over today. You could've dropped the dresses off at the shop, and you know it. What didn't you want to say to me there?"

Beth wrinkled her nose at me.

"Why would you say that?"

I put my hands on my hips.

"Because I've known you since we were 6."

"Fine. I did have a couple of things that I didn't want to say around Emmie."

"Why?"

"Because they've bothered me, I guess."

I wasn't following her.

"Beth, just spit it out."

"I told you that Mama went to get her hair fixed the other day."

"Yes, and she dropped the bombshell about Peggy and Jimmy's split."

"Yeah, well that's not the only bombshell she dropped on me."

"What are you talking about, Beth?"

"Mama's hairdresser is also Drew's mother's hairdresser."

I narrowed my eyes at her.

"So?"

"Well, she is under the impression that you and Drew are talking about working things out."

I closed my eyes and shook my head.

"Stop it. No, that's not happening, and where did she get that idea?"

"That's what I wanted to ask you."

"Drew and I are divorced. It's over."

"That's not what she thinks."

"I bet she loves that idea. She never forgave us for not having children. I was not on her favorite person list," I paused. "I've seen him several times, and he has acted like he wants to ask me out. He's been super nice to me. He's brought me breakfast at my shop."

I proceeded to tell her about his most recent visit and what Jimmy had left me taped under my desk.

"Well somewhere in there, Drew has gotten the idea that you are interested in getting back together with him."

I took a deep breath.

"Emmie said something similar, but he ended it. He doesn't get the chance to start it over."

"Finally."

"What are you talking about?"

"Grace, you finally have some fire in your voice concerning Drew. I'm glad you're angry."

"Being angry doesn't do me any good. I'm not. I'm just frustrated with everyone in this town wanting to be involved in my love life," I said as I started to head to her door. "Was that the only reason you dragged me over here today?"

"Not the only one. I have one other thing. Mama said that she thinks Steve Mathis is after Peggy for fiscal reasons rather than physical ones."

"Is anyone surprised by that, Beth? I knew that Peggy came from money, and I was sure she squirreled it away from Jimmy, especially knowing Jimmy's habits."

"True."

"But I don't know if that's enough to kill Jimmy over? Especially if she was divorcing him."

"Was he divorcing her though, Grace? I'm not so sure. Jimmy might not have had his name on all of Peggy's accounts, but he did have access to them through her. I'm not an expert in law, but as long as they were married, could they keep their assets separate?"

"I have no idea how to answer that, either, but I can't imagine someone like Steve Mathis killing anyone. He looks like the type who'd hire someone to do his dirty work."

Beth gave me an odd look. I wasn't sure if she wanted to laugh or cry at that remark.

"What's wrong, Beth?"

"Are you going to see Peggy tonight?"

I made a face, and she laughed.

"Mama has been calling me today. She's made several lemon pound cakes. She has one for Trevor, and one for Emmie. She wants me to go over to see Peggy tonight. What about you?"

"Yes, Mama has made her sweet potato soufflé, and we're going. It could be interesting, don't you think?"

I smiled at her.

"Maybe. Are you ready to go now?"

"What time is it? Isn't it too early?"

Beth wrinkled her nose.

"It's not too early at all. Knox's mother has the boys for me so I can go over to Peggy's tonight."

"We might as well get it over with, I suppose."

She laughed.

"Before we leave, there's one other thing Mama told me yesterday, and I wonder if it means anything."

"What was it?"

"Well, my Uncle Ted, Mama's brother, is a lawyer in Atlanta. He knew Steve Mathis from his high school days in Augusta. Five or six of his friends said Mathis had an investment scheme going. He asked them to each invest $100,000, which they did against their better judgement. He's a smooth talker from what I hear. It started with $100,000, but he kept asking for more money all while promising huge returns. They cut him off. For this group of people, $100,000 is small change. They considered pressing charges, but then they started acting afraid. When my uncle pressed them, they refused to talk to him about it. Nothing ever came of it."

"Did Jimmy and Peggy have a lot of money? I mean, really? I didn't think they were super wealthy. Plus, he had spending and gambling problems."

"Peggy came from money. She had property, stocks, and cash from her parents. They were big investors and left her their fortune. She's made some shrewd investments according to Mama. And she doesn't spend like Jimmy does. She watches money closely. That's the reason she always put him in the doghouse when it came to an addition to his antique gun collection. And back to what you asked earlier about if their finances were separate, I'm pretty sure she has nothing to do with his business. Her parents didn't want her to marry Jimmy, and they didn't want her giving him any of her money. He had to build that business on his own., and I think he's always kept her separated from it."

"You know all this stuff and never say anything."

"It didn't seem to matter until now," she said with a confused look.

"Makes me feel even worse for Jimmy."

"Well, you know he's had his own problems with gambling."

"I know, but he's such a good guy. Was such a good guy."

"He was nice, but he wasn't perfect."

"No one is perfect, not even you, Beth," I laughed. "So, you think that Steve Mathis was trying to get Peggy's money, not her heart."

"Yeah, plus Peggy has a different group of people he could potentially scam."

"I really don't like this guy, but why would Steve Mathis kill Jimmy?"

"Well, if Jimmy found out about his plan to steal Peggy's money - and who knows who else's - Jimmy might've tried to stop Steve or warn people about him. That could cost him a lot of money," she said.

"True. All I saw was Steve's photo on his website. He looks like a member of the mafia," I said and laughed uneasily. Beth didn't join in my laughter and glanced around. "Seriously, Beth? Is he?"

She shrugged her shoulders.

"Ties to organized crime? Your guess is as good as mine, but after what Mama says, it wouldn't surprise me in the least, Grace."

"I wonder if he'll be there tonight?"

"I guess you and I are about to find out. Want to take my car?"

"I don't have any food to take."

"We'll stop by Wife Saver and get some fried chicken."

"Perfect. Thanks for the dress. It's so pretty. I might take a little while to return it," I said with a smile.

"Honestly, it looks better on you than it did me. I was thinking about just letting you have it anyway," she said as I picked up the dress that she'd placed in a garment bag. I probably didn't want to know the price tag on it.

"You don't have to do that."

She smiled.

"You or Catholic Social Services Thrift Shop. Take your pick."

"Fine, you drive a hard bargain, Beth," I said as we walked over to put my dress in my car.

"And Grace, you're going to be fine. I promise."

"Thanks. I need you more than you know."

We stopped and got some fried chicken and macaroni and

cheese to take to Peggy. When we arrived, there were several cars in the driveway, including Mama's.

I wasn't sure what I expected to see when I got there. I knocked on the door because Beth was holding the box of chicken. I had the macaroni and cheese. Mama opened the door.

"Peggy's in the sunroom. Beth, Libby is out there with her," she said. Libby was Beth's mom. I hugged Mama. I could tell she'd been crying.

"How's Peggy?" I asked.

"About as good as can be expected," she replied, taking the food from me and directing Beth to bring the chicken into the kitchen. Most of the food would be for after the funeral, but as I peeked into the dining room, I noticed there was some food out on the table already.

People milled around her dining room as a casual line formed. I looked around the house and saw Becca standing inside the living room with her boyfriend, Clint. Becca had had a string of boyfriends, from what I'd heard. She never seemed to get too serious about them, except for Clint, who had driven a truck at one time but was out of work. He was tall and skinny, and I'd gathered that Jimmy didn't like him much.

When I had asked him how Becca was, Jimmy had gritted his teeth and shook his head disdainfully as he talked about her no-good boyfriend. He thought she could do better than a boozing, conniving trucker. Jimmy thought Clint was after his money. It was clear she did not have her father's approval. I wondered if Peggy shared that feeling since Becca wasn't at her mother's side but was at her boyfriend's side instead.

On the other hand, Jimmy's son, Jake, was standing in the sunroom with Peggy. He had recently gotten a divorce after going through rehab for the third or fourth time. He had two small daughters.

"Do you see who else I see?" Beth asked.

I glanced at her and followed her gaze. I could see into the sunroom. Steve Mathis was there – in the flesh.

Beth's mama walked out of the sunroom as we stood in the dining room. Her lips were pursed. She wasn't happy, and it had nothing to do with Jimmy being dead.

She walked toward her daughter and gave her a hug.

"The nerve of that man," I could hear her saying as she embraced Beth.

I bit my lip to keep myself from laughing. My eyes darted into the other direction, so I didn't meet Libby's gaze. I was sure she would've scolded me as though I was a little girl.

"Glad to see you made it," she said to Beth. The tone conveyed more of a message than the words. It was a snide way of saying "I'm glad to see I taught you Southern graces and manners."

"Of course, I'm here, Mama," Beth answered. "Jimmy was our friend."

Beth's mother lowered her voice.

"Can you believe he's here? Jimmy's not even in the grave, and that man's at Peggy's house."

"So disrespectful," commented my mother, who had found her way into the conversation.

"Do we really know what was going on there?" I asked.

Both Libby and my mother glared at me.

"Doesn't matter. It has the appearance of evil. And sometimes, that's enough," Libby said.

Steve didn't seem uncomfortable, but he did look completely out of place. He did have a Marlon Brando "Godfather" air about him. I couldn't quite pinpoint what made me think that.

"Are you ready to leave, Lottie?" she asked.

"Yes, I've done all I can," my mother replied and turned to me. "Grace, I've got some pound cake for you to take to Emmie and Trevor. It's in a cooler in my car."

"I'll come with you," I said, glancing at her then Beth, who handed me her keys.

I followed them out to the car and got the cooler to put into

Beth's.

"Watch out for that Steve Mathis," my mother warned me.

"You don't have to worry there, Mama. He's scary."

"He's more than scary. I think he's dangerous," she said. "I used to know him a long time ago. He always liked the thrill of the chase, fast cars, dangerous drag races, picking fights."

Libby nodded at me.

"He was never one to turn down a dare," she interjected and then turned to Mama. "Do you remember the time he challenged Jimmy to drag race down Washington Road?"

My mother's mouth dropped, and she covered it with her hand.

"Oh, my goodness. I'd totally forgotten about that. It's a wonder both of them didn't get killed."

"What are you talking about?"

My mother turned to look at me.

"They played chicken and drove down the wrong side of the street. It's a wonder they didn't kill anyone," Mama said.

"Well, it was at 3 a.m. so there weren't as many people out at that time of night."

"Doesn't matter."

"All I remember is Peggy going out of her mind," Mama said to Libby before turning back to talk to me. "I'll see you tomorrow."

I nodded. I knew we'd probably run into each other at the funeral home. When I returned inside, I noticed Beth standing in a corner talking with a friend of ours from high school. I lingered near the door, smiling at people as they left and making small talk. I wandered into the room where Becca and Clint were. I smiled at them, and Becca acknowledged me with a nod. I noticed them watching Steve Mathis. Becca's boyfriend uncomfortably fidgeted in the chair.

"I can't believe he had the nerve to show up," Becca said.

"How much longer do we have to stay here? This creeps me out," Clint asked, clearly annoyed.

"I may have to stay the rest of the day."

"I need a cigarette," Clint got up and walked out of the room. Becca glanced at me and followed him.

It wasn't long before Steve wandered into the room. I'd found a corner near a window and was gazing outside when I noticed him standing nearby.

"Are you Grace?" he asked.

"Well, yes," I said. I couldn't lie.

He smiled.

"I overheard someone call you that. You made the flowers I ordered for Peggy the other day."

"Yes, sir. That's the arrangement over there," I said pointing to the flowers on a table in the room we were in.

"You did a wonderful job," he said. "The dahlias are more striking than I thought. The colors are amazing."

I wasn't sure how to take him. I'd already painted him as an enemy and now he was complementing me.

"Thank you. I love those too. People appreciate flowers. It brings joy even in sadness."

"I hope that they brought Peggy a little joy. She's had many sad days recently through no fault of her own.

I didn't respond.

"Shame that this had to happen to Jimmy," he continued. "Bad timing."

Bad timing? That statement made the hair on my neck stand on end. What did that mean – bad timing? Was Jimmy's death an inconvenience to him? I waited for him to say something else.

"We were in the middle of a business deal," he said.

I smiled weakly as a wave of nausea overtook me. I wanted to say, "How inconsiderate of Jimmy to be murdered and put you out of a business deal," but I bit my tongue and thought of something else.

"It's very sad," I said. "Jimmy has been a friend of the family for many years. He was always buying flowers for Peggy. She loved them so."

"Yes, she's fond of flowers. It's nice to meet you, Grace," he abruptly ended the conversation.

"Thank you, Mr. Mathis."

"Steve," he responded.

"Steve," I replied.

It didn't take long for Beth to be at my side.

"What was that about?" she asked.

"I don't really know. He made it sound like it was an inconvenience for Jimmy to die and that he was annoyed."

"Oh," she responded.

We merged into the sunroom. People didn't stay long. They gave their sentiments and their hugs and moved out of the way for the next in line to do the same. I noticed Peggy was standing near the window and the beautiful hibiscus Jimmy told me he'd given her. There was one bloom on it. It was a rich orange, edged in yellow. Jake stood behind his mother. Jake was tall and gangly. He wore a black pair of pants with an ill-fitting white shirt. He was deathly pale and seemed to be somewhere besides the room we were standing in. He didn't acknowledge anyone's presence. I stared at him for a while, trying not to be obvious. He was sweating profusely, but it was cold inside the Hughes' home. I also noticed his hands seemed to shake.

"Grace and Beth, it's so good to see both of you," Peggy said as she hugged each of us.

She'd put on extra makeup for the occasion and was wearing a black dress with a strand of pearls.

"Is there anything we can do for you?"

"No, but thank you for asking," she said.

I watched Peggy as she talked with Beth. I noticed she kept glancing out of the room to where Steve was. She was unnerved, but I was sure it wasn't related to Jimmy's death. It seemed like it had more to do with Steve.

"Are you sure?" Beth asked.

"No, dear. There's nothing you can do," she glanced at Steve again and drew in a deep breath.

Beth wasn't buying it, and I didn't either. Neither of us really knew how to help Peggy.

"You know how to reach us if you need us," she said.

"Thank you both for coming. Give your boys a hug for me," she said. "It's good to see you again, Grace."

As we walked out of the sunroom, I glanced at Steve. I didn't understand why he looked so smug. We were silent until we got into Beth's car.

"Okay, what do you have?" she asked.

"I don't like Steve Mathis," I said relaying the brief conversation plus what our mothers had said.

"Neither do I," she said. "Did you see Jake? He looked like he was going through withdrawals again."

"How many times has he been to rehab?"

"I can't answer that, but he looks awful."

"They all do, Beth."

"I noticed Peggy's silver tea service was missing."

"I didn't see any of the silver pieces that used to be in her china cabinet."

"It was empty, Grace. I wonder what that means?"

"I don't know. Maybe Jake was pawning it for his gambling debts or drug habit."

Beth shook her head.

"This gets sadder by the minute."

"I know."

"What are your plans for the rest of the night?"

""I have to deliver some pound cake, but I think I just want to go home."

"I don't blame you. You can give Emmie her pound cake in the morning."

"Agreed."

12

I had no idea how other parts of the country dealt with deaths and funerals, but in the South, we fed everyone casseroles, fried chicken, cake, and pie. We visited with the family before the funeral, after the funeral, and at their homes. My mother got a lot of use out of her pound cake recipe. I didn't have a signature funeral dish like Beth's mom and mine had. And my mother always made extra, usually for me and for Emmie.

Emmie was ready for her pound cake as soon as she got into the shop. She cut a piece of it and put it on a plate.

"Do you want any?"

I shook my head "no."

"It's too early in the morning for that. Besides, I thought you were on a diet."

Emmie laughed.

"It's never too early in the morning for this. Your mother makes the best pound cake. Who can diet with this around? We really should have her go into the cake business, and we could corner the wedding market," she said.

I laughed.

"She does it out of love. I don't think she wants to start a business."

"I know, sweetie, but all of Augusta needs your mom's pound cake."

"That's not exactly the right type of cake for weddings."

"People would change their minds once the lemon melts in their mouths," she said

Most of Friday was business as usual. No phone calls from Drew, which was odd considering I'd been at Peggy's the night before. And there were no mysterious packages taped under my desk. Nothing out of the ordinary for most of the day.

We were busy with more funeral arrangements and getting ready for the weekend's weddings.

Trevor met me at the apartment after I'd closed up shop and taken care of the evening's brides. I'd put on my best black funeral dress. The last time I'd worn it was at his mother's funeral. With it came the requisite strand of pearls and black pumps.

There was a good crowd at the funeral home. Jimmy had done some good things in his life. When Jake was little, Jimmy coached his little league baseball teams and was a scoutmaster. He was a member of the Kiwanis Club and the Rotary Club, faithfully going to their regular meetings. He volunteered for his church's annual Christmas tree sale to raise money for the soup kitchen and homeless ministries.

I'd already signed the book when I was delivering flowers. I was getting used to signing just my name.

A slideshow played with pictures of Jimmy as a little boy, his high school graduation, his and Peggy's wedding, with their children. I glanced around the main lobby. There was a line into the viewing room where the family would be. Trevor and I took our place in line. He didn't say much, but I noticed him watching me.

When Beth and Knox arrived, we got out of line and moved to be with them. Emmie came in less than five minutes later. She gave me a hug.

"So, what are we looking for?" she whispered in my ear.

I pulled back and scowled at her. She laughed and rolled her eyes at me.

I noticed Trevor's suspicious glance again. I tried to shift the conversation.

"I got a couple of orders in after you left, and a bride called about a September wedding," I said.

Before long, the gender segregation of the conversation had set in. Knox and Trevor talked about medical things and Trevor's brothers, while Emmie, Beth, and I talked about flowers, weddings, and what people were wearing to the funeral home. Actually, there wasn't much talking about that last one. That was a subtle form of conversation with various glances, eyebrow raises, scowls, a few wrinkled noses, and some definite shakes of the head. In our more than two decades of friendship, Emmie, Beth, and I had our own form of nonverbal communication. We knew exactly what the others were thinking by a simple or not-so-simple facial expression.

It took about 30 minutes before we'd made it to the viewing room. The line of visitors was so long. Peggy refused to look me in the eye. Steve wasn't there. Jake's face was blank and distant. Becca seemed annoyed, and her boyfriend, Clint, stayed outside and smoked cigarettes for most of the evening. I also met Jimmy's sisters and several of his nieces and nephews. I recognized them from Peggy's the night before, but I didn't know who they were then. They seemed like nice people as far as 30 seconds of "I'm sorry for your loss" could register.

There wasn't anything unusual. There were no smoking guns, no family fights, nothing that would've signaled our killer was in the room. I didn't see Debbie, but I knew a couple of the mechanics who'd worked on my car and my floral delivery van. They were there, and they seemed shaken. I did not see Billy, the mechanic who'd been on the phone with Debbie when I took the wreath there.

The five of us exited the funeral home together.

"Would you like to come to our house for coffee?" Beth asked.

I shook my head.

"I think I'm done for the day."

"Yeah, Beth. I'm tired. Someone deprived me of my sleep earlier this week and I haven't caught up yet," Emmie said, staring at me. "I think I'm going to have some more of Lottie's pound cake and take a long bubble bath. Maybe I'll eat it in my tub."

"What about you, Trevor?" Beth asked.

"I think I'll take Grace home and get myself mentally ready for tomorrow. A funeral and a dog-and-pony show all in one day. I can't wait," he said sarcastically.

"Edward seems excited about your party tomorrow night," Knox interjected.

"I'm sure he does," Trevor answered blandly. I knew what he meant, but I wasn't sure Knox did.

Knox laughed.

"You know he speaks very highly of you. He hasn't stopped talking about how you took the time to be with your mother during the last few months of her life, and how you worked at the clinic."

Trevor looked at the ground.

"I know they are hard on you," Knox continued. "But I think their hearts are in the right place. They want you to be happy."

"Thank you, Knox. I appreciate that," Trevor reached out to shake Knox's hand. "I'll see you and Beth tomorrow."

"Looking forward to it," Beth said as she linked arms with Knox, and they headed to their car.

Trevor and I walked to his car without talking. Once inside, however, he turned on the car and the air conditioning before turning to look at me.

"Are you okay, Grace?" he asked me.

"I'm just drained, Trevor. This has been a hard week."

He didn't answer right away.

"So, I guess you aren't making that fresh salsa for me tonight?" he asked lightheartedly.

"I'd forgotten about that. The past few days have seemed like months."

"I know what you mean."

"I really feel like I need to go to my house or apartment or whatever you want to call it. I need to be at home. I can't explain why.

You can come inside. I don't know if I have any food. There might be some ice cream. I think I might have some watermelon."

He smiled.

"I'll take you home. I know you're nervous about tomorrow night. But I'll let you in on a little secret," he took a breath. "I'm probably more nervous about this than you are."

"Really? Why?"

"You were right when you said I wanted their approval. I know that. I was the baby of the family. They all tried to take some type of superior role to me as we were growing up. I couldn't play with them because I was too little. I couldn't do things with them when they were at home. When I went off to college and medical school and finally came back, they never saw me as an adult; they've always seen me as a child."

I touched his hand.

"Thank you, Grace, for agreeing to go with me. I really need the moral support, whether you realize it or not."

"Of course," I said.

Once we got back to Zack's house, he walked me to my door.

"Do you want to come inside?" I asked.

"I do, but I think I should go home. You're distracted."

"I am?"

He pursed his lips and nodded.

"Did you get all your spying done?" he asked; there was a hint of something in his voice. I wasn't sure if it was anger or sarcasm because it was so subtle.

"Spying?" I countered.

"You did your social duty, but you were also spying for Drew," that statement wasn't as subtle. I could hear the faint anger in his voice. I didn't respond right away. He didn't look like Drew did when Drew was upset. There wasn't a steely glint in his eye, and his jaw wasn't clenched. But there was the slightest of bulges at his temple.

He waited for me to say something.

"I wouldn't call it spying."

"What would you call it, then?" he asked.

"I watch and observe. I've always liked to watch people."

"And then you report back to Drew? Is that how it works?" I could hear the repressed anger in his voice.

I stared at him and thought carefully before I answered. I was surprised at him because he never acted that way.

"If I saw anything that would help Drew find out who killed Jimmy, then yes. I'd call Drew," I whispered.

"That's spying."

"Why are you so upset, Trevor?"

"I don't understand why you insist on helping him."

"I want to find out who killed Jimmy."

"That's Drew's job, not yours," his tone was even, but I could tell he wasn't happy with me.

"Drew's not omniscient. And I don't understand why everyone gets upset."

"Because he's put you in danger more than one time. And you've put yourself in danger more than one time."

"I'm not doing anything."

"Maybe not yet, but you have. You've tried to solve these cases on your own."

"No, Trevor. I haven't. You sound like my mother."

"Wise woman, maybe you should listen to her."

Now he was getting me angry; his tone was becoming more biting with each phrase.

"I wasn't going to tell you this, but Jimmy left me a stack of papers taped underneath my desk drawer. He dragged me into this. And now that I'm in the middle, I want to see it through to the end."

He didn't say anything right away. He put his hands on his hips and stared at me.

"I don't want you getting hurt, Grace, and every time you're around Drew, you get agitated. And you've been placed in dangerous situations."

He touched my arm.

"Look, I know you've never understood. No one has. I don't willingly search out a crime scene and think 'Oh, I'll meddle in police business where I have no business being.' It doesn't work that way."

He glanced at the ground.

"I need to leave," he said.

"Trevor, are we having a fight?"

The thought scared me. We hadn't had one of those. Even the first time we dated as teenagers we didn't really fight then. We always got along well.

He glanced back and smiled softly.

"No, I'm not fighting with you. You and I have differing opinions. You have a right to yours, and I have a right to mine. Since we are friends, I feel that gives me a right to express my opinion, and frankly, your behavior scares me at times. You're too close to this situation to see things clearly. I don't want to see you get hurt - or worse - because you were an innocent bystander caught in the line of fire, so to speak. What bothers me the most is the man who keeps telling you he doesn't want anything to happen to you is the one who continually puts you in danger. And you let him."

I didn't respond.

"I need to leave. I hope you'll still go with me tomorrow night. If not, I understand."

That last comment stung. He started to turn to walk down the stairs, but I touched his arm to keep him from going.

"Why wouldn't I go with you? Of course, I'll be there." I said. I could feel tears welling up after his words had stung me.

He smiled faintly.

"I admire that nothing stops you once you've made up your mind to do something, but reason doesn't always have a chance against that determination," he said.

"I'm sorry you think that. I'm not chasing after anyone, just providing information."

"I'll call you in the morning," he said without acknowledging my comment.

"Good night, Trevor."

"Good night, Grace," he said giving me a brief, stiff hug.

I walked inside and immediately took off my shoes. I was ready to get out of my funeral uniform, but I needed some sweet tea first. I pulled the pitcher from the refrigerator and poured a large glass. I heard a knock on the door. At first, I thought it might be Trevor, but I opened the door to see my sister-in-law, Sarah, standing there.

"Hey. This came for you a couple of days ago. Blame it on mom brain, but I totally forgot about it until I was cleaning this afternoon," she said as she handed me a brown envelope. I gasped as I saw the handwriting. "I'm so sorry."

I nodded.

"When did it arrive?"

"What's today? Friday? I think it was Wednesday. I got it out of the mailbox. With Zack out of town, my brain is on overload. I put it down because one of the kids was into something they shouldn't have been."

"Thank you."

"Mommy!"

I could hear yelling outside.

"Duty calls," she sighed, rushing out the door. "Coming!"

I stared at the envelope. It was postmarked Tuesday. Jimmy died Monday. I sucked in a deep breath as I debated opening it. It felt like there was something inside it, and not just a piece of paper. I felt my heart sinking as I opened the clasp and pulled out a key. There was also a note.

Little lady. I wasn't completely honest with you tonight. You were right about me being afraid. I am. I'm not the person you think I am, and I appreciate your kindness more than you know. My life isn't worth living anymore, not without Peggy, not without my kids, and not without my businesses. I know you don't understand. And I'm sorry to do this to you. I'm sorry I left you information at your office, but I trust you, Grace. I trust you more than I trust my own family. There's some information the police will need. I've hidden it in a place that no one would think to look because not too many people even know about it. You'll find it there. Here's the address. Call Cal first. He'll be expecting you.

Tears were streaming down my cheeks. No wonder he was upset. He had planned to kill himself, but Drew wouldn't be investigating a suicide. I knew that if I went to this address alone, I'd have several people upset with me. Drew, Trevor, my mother, Emmie – they'd all have something to say about it. But I wasn't about to hand over this information unless Drew let me go with him. I stared at my phone. I hesitated calling Drew; instead, I pulled up a map of the address. It was at the lake. I wondered what could be at the lake.

I called Drew.

"Grace?" he answered with a question.

"Don't take this the wrong way, but I need you to come to my apartment."

He chuckled but took his time in responding.

"I was hoping you'd call. Did you just get back from the funeral home?"

"Yeah, but there's something you need to see. I'm not talking about it on the phone."

"I'll be there shortly," he said.

I sat down at my table and covered my face with my hands. I wondered what he'd left for me to find. He left some detailed instructions about where to find the item in question. I needed to change before Drew arrived. I didn't need to wear the black dress I'd worn to the funeral home. I threw on a pair of jean shorts, a T-shirt and a pair of tennis shoes.

It didn't take him long to get to the apartment. I opened the door and let him in. He looked around.

"No Emmie to protect you?" he asked sarcastically.

"Do I need protecting, Drew?"

"You could've fooled me the other day."

I ignored his comment as I turned and walked toward the table where I'd left the letter and key. "Jimmy mailed this to me.

Sarah said it arrived on Wednesday, but she's been distracted with the kids because Zack is out of town."

I picked it up and held it out to him.

I watched as he read it.

"I guess you aren't turning this over to me, are you?"

"Not a chance. It was sent to me. And Cal is expecting me, apparently."

"Have you called him?"

"I was waiting on you before I did that."

"Call him, and you and I will take a trip to this address. You've looked it up, I take it."

I grinned at him.

"Of course, I did."

"I need to make my own call while you do that, Grace."

I called the number and a man with a thick Southern accent answered.

"Cal?" I asked.

"Yes, ma'am," he replied.

"I'm Grace Ward."

"I've been expecting your call. Are you on your way?"

"Yes, give us about 30 minutes."

"Drew Ward coming with you?" he asked.

"Yes."

"See you in 30."

I ended the call and looked at Drew.

"He's expecting you, too."

Drew pursed his lips and nodded at me.

"Well, then, let's go. I'm driving," he said. "You can give me directions."

The last time Drew and I were in a vehicle together for any length of time was nearly a year ago when he and I went to Edisto. That was a great week together. We enjoyed the surf, sand, quiet meals, and each other. I had to stop that line of thinking. It would get me into trouble especially considering his renewed interest in me., but there was no going back to what might've been. It was too late.

"Penny?" he asked; his abbreviated version of "a penny for your thoughts?"

I tried to think of something to say. I certainly didn't want to tell him the truth.

"Just wondering about the mess Jimmy got himself into."

"I'm working on unraveling it. It goes deeper than we imagined."

"I wonder what he left for us to find at the lake, Drew. I mean, he already left a lot of paperwork at my office."

I rambled, but there was a question I really needed to ask him.

"He did, but those were copies. I'm wondering if he's left you ledgers, cancelled checks, or some other paper trail. Jimmy was old school. He may have had some things on computer, but you know he had paper."

I didn't respond right away. We were getting close to the summer solstice, so the days were long. It was approaching sunset, and we were heading west. The brilliant oranges, reds, and pinks consumed the evening sky. It was beautiful and was a nice - albeit brief - distraction from what weighed heavily on my mind.

"Drew, his note made it sound like he was going to commit suicide," my voice caught in my throat as I said that.

"It did, but I can promise you one thing, Grace. Jimmy's death was no suicide."

There was an uncomfortable pause.

"Unless Jimmy was a contortionist and could shoot himself in the back of the head," Drew continued.

"Oh," I said. "I've tried not to think about it."

"Yeah. I don't want to fill your mind with pictures, Grace, so that's all I'll say about that topic. Anything else you want to know?"

"If you think this trip has more to do with embezzlement, why are you taking it with me?"

"Because you don't need to be taking it alone. And I never

said that it was just about Debbie. I don't know what this trip has to do with. Debbie will be in jail soon enough. I already told you that. I can't tell you what all the charges will be because I don't know yet. There's not any forensic evidence to connect her to Jimmy's death."

There was a lot of silence for the rest of the trip. He asked about the funeral home, but there wasn't much to tell. I did tell him about Beth and my visit to the Hughes residence. He was interested in how the family acted and what they said. I also told him about the missing silver pieces.

From there, the conversation lulled. I stared out the window wondering where we were headed. I didn't know what type of place Jimmy had at the lake. It wasn't anything we'd ever talked about. As we drove out Washington Road, we passed rows upon rows of towering pines on our way to Appling in Columbia County.

We turned onto a dirt driveway surrounded by more of those massive trees. It wound around until we arrived at a small cabin. Next to the wooden structure was a metal building. As we pulled onto the concrete pad behind a battered Ford pick-up truck, a man wearing a baseball cap, a T-shirt with a beer logo on it and a pair of blue jeans stepped out the front door.

I got out of the vehicle and waited for Drew to walk around to me.

"Are you Cal?" Drew asked.

"Yes, sir, I am," he said. "You must be Grace, and you must be Drew."

He identified both of us and reached out to shake hands with us.

"This is Jimmy's fishing shack. That's what he called it. He came up here when he was sad and lonely, which was a lot over the past few months," Cal said as he walked toward the metal building. He looked at me.

"Jimmy's let me live out here rent-free for about five years. I watch things for him, make sure no one goes hunting on the property. That sort of thing. He has three acres out here. I can go anywhere on the property, but I'm not allowed in the garage unless he's here. As a matter of fact, I don't even have a key to this building. You're the one that has that key."

"I do?" I asked slowly, confused by all of this.

"Yes, ma'am. Mr. Jimmy told me he was mailing it to you. He didn't tell me why."

I pulled the key out of my pocket and stared at the building. There was a rolltop garage door and a side door. I went to the side door to see if the key fit. It did, of course. I walked in and flipped the light switch. It was a working garage with lifts and all of the tools and machinery to repair cars. There was also an office area as though Jimmy had done business in the spot.

I heard Drew gasp.

"Cal, is that…" he started to ask, pointing at the gold car with black accents.

"A 1968 Camaro Z28 sports coupe. Yes sir, it is. It's a mighty fine machine."

"That is one amazing machine," Drew gushed as he walked around the gold muscle car. I wasn't impressed; however, for Drew to react that way, I figured it was something special.

"Jimmy said that was always his dream car. He bought it a while ago, and it was a mess. He showed me photos. The body was all tore up, and the engine was shot. Jimmy worked on it religiously. That was his baby. The engine sure sounds sweet now."

"What a vehicle. I've always wanted one of those," he said to my surprise. I never knew that.

Drew was sidetracked. I put my hands in my pockets, and I watched as the two of them circle the Camaro. After a few moments, Drew started looking around the building. I pulled the letter from my pocket. It gave details of where to find whatever it was we were looking for. I glanced toward the back of the garage. The note mentioned lockers, and there was a series of numbers, which I assumed was a combination to a lock. My attention was drawn back to Drew, who seemed to be staring at something in a corner opposite me.

"Cal, two things for you. We were allowed to come here. Is that correct? We didn't force our way in," Drew said.

"Yes, sir. Jimmy told me you were coming."

I stared at Drew.

"And you don't mind us looking around."

"Not one bit. I've got nothing to hide. Jimmy told me to let you come out. I don't know what will happen to me now that he's gone. He was a good man. But my instructions were to let you look around. He actually wrote it down. He said something about making everything legal," I hadn't noticed Cal was holding an envelope. Another envelope. I was so tired of envelopes. He handed it to Drew. He took a few steps away from Cal before opening it and studying its contents.

"It's even on letterhead. I had no idea Jimmy had letterhead," Drew laughed. He continued to walk. It seemed as though something had caught his eye. There was a box shoved into a corner. I could see a piece of material sticking out of it. He knelt down to take a closer look, but he was careful not to disturb any of the contents. He stood up and took his phone from his pocket.

"Hey, Kenny. About our call from earlier, I need someone with Columbia County," he said, giving the address. He put on the latex gloves that he'd brought with him.

I walked closer to Drew.

"What's going on?" I asked.

Drew pointed at the box. As I peered at it, I saw the reason for the call. Lying on top of what looked like a blood-stained shirt was a gun. That didn't make any sense to me if Drew was thinking what I thought he was thinking. How could the gun have gotten here?

"Is that…" I started to ask Drew.

With his gloves on, he picked up the weapon, eyeing it closely. He turned to look at me.

"The gun that killed Jimmy?" he finished my sentence. "It's

possible. This is an antique; maybe it was part of Jimmy's collection. They sure don't make them like this anymore. This is an absolutely beautiful gun."

I stared at it. I knew what he meant. He was looking at the craftsmanship, and even though, I wasn't close to it, I could see that this was no ordinary gun. That was definitely something Jimmy would have in his collection.

"Drew, what is the grip made of?"

"It looks like pearl, Grace."

My breath caught in my throat. I remembered Jimmy telling me about a grip inlaid with mother-of-pearl. That gun put him in the doghouse for several weeks. But more than that, the fact that the gun was here of all places, meant the killer was one of Jimmy's family members. Drew didn't pick up the shirt, but I could tell it was a T-shirt, not the type of clothing Peggy would wear. Jake or Becca? That couldn't be right. I couldn't believe his own flesh and blood killed him. I felt nauseated and found a corner of the room to sit down. Poor Jimmy. I felt even worse because he was always so nice to me. I should've done more to help him when I knew he was in trouble.

I glanced up to see Drew looking at me.

"I don't understand," I said.

He didn't answer. Instead, he turned to Cal, who looked as stunned as I felt.

"When was the last time Jimmy was here?" he asked Cal.

Cal glanced at the box, me, and then back at Drew.

"He was here Sunday. We spent some time working on the car, and he even took me for a ride in it," Cal answered with a grin. "He'd never let anyone sit in this car."

"When did he tell you that we were coming out here?"

"Monday afternoon. He called and told me that he'd left something in the garage, and then I heard about his passing Tuesday. It shook me up really good," he said.

"Who else knows about this place?" Drew continued.

"Just his family as far as I know. I don't know anything about other keys. And I've never seen that gun before. I have hunting rifles, no handguns," he said. "You can check the house. I don't have anything to hide."

"Have you ever seen any of Jimmy's family here?"

"Not recently. Maybe when I first moved here, but I've been here five years now. Peggy didn't take to the out-of-doors. She liked a/c and sweet tea and all the niceties this place doesn't have."

"Jake or Becca?"

"Jake used to come out a lot, but he didn't like that I stayed here. He and Jimmy worked on this car together a lot. But I think he's been in rehab more in the past year than he's been out. He hasn't been here. And Becca came out a couple of times with that boyfriend of hers last fall."

"No one else?"

"No, sir. No one else."

"Cal, did you see anyone here Monday late or Tuesday?" Drew continued to ask his questions. I was listening, but I was still stunned. Becca or Jake killed Jimmy? Or I guess it could've been Becca's boyfriend, Clint. I wonder what he had against Jimmy. I knew the two of them didn't get along. I mean, I knew they were a dysfunctional family. At least, I'd learned that over the past few days. I never imagined his life was perfect; but this was a far cry from what I thought it might be. I could faintly hear Cal's voice in the background. His thick Southern drawl cut into my thoughts.

"No, sir. Monday nights, I usually watch wrestling. This Monday, I was out on the lake fishing for a while before I came in and washed up. I fell asleep with the TV on. On Tuesday, I went fishing, and I was on the lake from sun-up until about 10 a.m. Came back and cleaned my haul. I put some in the freezer and had fish for lunch.

"And no one has been here since Jimmy came out Sunday."

"Not that I know of. If they came, they did it while I was on the lake or asleep."

"And there's no video surveillance or anything?"

He laughed.

"Nah. The only thing on video would be a few deer and maybe a possum or two."

"Just checking," Drew said.

His phone started buzzing.

"Hey Kenny. Yeah, just come straight back," he said. "Kenny is with Columbia County. He lives down the street. I needed him."

This was dragging out longer than I'd intended. It was getting late. I was tired, hungry, and on edge. And this nightmare was getting worse. I'd forgotten about the locker. I didn't care what was in it. I was stunned and sick with the thought that one of Jimmy's family members might have pulled the trigger. I couldn't think of too many things more horrible than killing your parent. Within a few minutes, there were headlights as a pickup truck pulled into the yard. Then Kenny, the deputy from the neighboring county, walked into the garage. I stood up and walked over to where Drew was.

"Long time no see, Drew," he said reaching out for Drew's hand.

"Good to see you. This is my" – he hesitated and looked at me. He looked back at Kenny before continuing. "This is my ex-wife, Grace."

He glanced at Drew then me and reached out to shake my hand.

"Ma'am," he said.

"She has the letter I was telling you about," Drew said. "Grace, would you show it to Kenny?"

I handed it to him for him to read over. Once he'd finished, he gave it back.

"And this is Cal, who has been kindly cooperating with us," Drew continued the formalities. "He's the caretaker out here, and he said Jimmy gave him the permission to let us in. Incidentally, he doesn't have the key to this building, but Grace does. Our murder victim mailed it to her before his death."

"I take it you found something besides whatever the murder victim left you," Kenny asked.

Drew motioned for Kenny to follow him to the box. They both crouched near the box as Kenny put on a pair of latex gloves.

"Looks like a bloody shirt and something shiny," Kenny said as he picked up the gun with his gloved hand. He held it up. "Wow, that is a beautiful gun."

"Yes, sir. That's something special, right there. I've been looking for one of those," Drew responded.

"You think this pertains to your case?"

"Could be. I need to take that with me."

Drew still had on his gloves. He'd put the gun back in the box, where we'd found it. Kenny handed him the gun and turned his attention back to the box as Drew took a closer look at the gun.

"Always happy to lend a hand. And what about this?" he asked as he pulled the blood-stained shirt out of the box. It was a large white T-shirt with an ad on it. As he held it up, I could see the blood spatters on it. I cringed and looked away. It looked too big for any of the current suspects to be wearing.

"I'll need that, too," Drew said. "Is there anything left inside the box?"

"No. Just those two things," Kenny examined the box. "The box is addressed to your victim, Jimmy Hughes."

"Work or home?"

"It's a 30901 ZIP."

"That's his work location."

"What else have you got for me, Drew?" Kenny asked.

Drew looked at me.

"Are you ready to look in that locker, Grace?" he asked.

I really didn't want to see inside. I didn't want to know anymore. Trevor was right about a few things. Even though this wasn't a dangerous situation in my eyes, it brought a lot of pain with it. It was hurting me, maybe not physically but definitely emotionally.

"Grace?" he prompted.

"No, I don't want to know what's in there."

He tilted his head to the side.

"Come on, Gracie. Let's look inside."

If I hadn't been so preoccupied with Jimmy's murder and narrowed suspect list, I probably would've bolted at his use of the nickname "Gracie," but I was too numb, sick, and heartbroken for it to register a response.

I held out the note.

"Here. You look."

He pushed it back to me.

"No, Jimmy dragged you into this for a reason. Let's find out what it is."

I scowled at Drew and walked to the set of lockers. There were six of them. A few of them had labels on them. – Jimmy, Peggy, Becca, Jake, as though they were there to hold the person's belongings. One was marked as miscellaneous and the other was marked as cleaning supplies. It was the cleaning supplies one that had a combination lock on it. I looked at my paper. The numbers were 22-34-15. I dialed the knob and with a click, it opened.

I took a breath. I wasn't sure what I was going to find. I didn't expect to find wads of cash or jewels or anything like that. I figured it would pertain to the money Debbie had stolen. Drew knew what he hoped was inside, and I thought that, too. But part of me wondered if there might be something else besides just documents.

Neither of us were completely wrong.

There were several leather-bound ledgers. Drew was right about Jimmy being old school. I stepped back and allowed Drew to remove them.

Once he'd taken the books out, I looked in the back of the locker. There was a small ring box and two more envelopes. I'd put on a pair of gloves as well. I picked up the box and opened it. It was a diamond ring. Nothing like the one Peggy had worn in recent years. It had a tiny diamond, if you could call it that. It wasn't much more than a chip. I looked at the envelopes; one was addressed to Peggy, and one was addressed to me.

I drew in a deep breath. I wasn't sure I could read another note from Jimmy, no matter what it said.

"What's the matter, Grace?" I heard Drew behind me.

I handed him the ring box and the two notes. I walked outside the shop into the sticky, hot summer night. The sun had long since gone down, and without the glow of streetlights, it was dark. I could see a few stars out, and the moon was bright. Since I couldn't see where I was going, I didn't go too far. I sucked in the June air. A soft albeit hot breeze gently kissed the tears on my cheeks. The hoot of an owl echoed in the distance, and the lightning bugs danced around in the sky.

I felt Drew walk up behind me. He didn't touch me, but I knew he was close.

"Are you okay?" he asked softly.

"You know I'm not okay, Drew," I said, not wanting to cry anymore, but knowing I couldn't stop.

I felt Drew step closer to me; his arms reaching around me. I turned and buried my face in his chest. He said nothing as I cried against him in the dark.

"I'm sorry. I have to stop doing that," I said as I backed away from him and walked further down the lake path. I just kept moving forward until I could see the moonlight shimmering off the top of the lake. There was a dock straight ahead, and I followed the path until I reached it. I moved to the end and sat, bringing my knees to my chest. Drew followed me and sat down next to me.

"I have a few more questions for Cal, and then we can leave. Okay?"

"Take your time, Drew. I don't want to go home right now anyway."

"Are you going to be all right while I go back?"

"Yes, I'll be fine."

"Here, I know you can't read in the dark, but this is addressed to you," he said as he held out the note from Jimmy.

I wasn't sure how long he stayed inside talking to Cal and Kenny.

I listened to the chirping of the crickets and the song of the frogs and gazed at the constellations as they emerged in the night sky. I realized how tired I was as I sat there. I wished I had a blanket to spread out onto the dock so I could rest there. Even though I didn't, I leaned back on the wooden planks and gazed into the sky.

It wasn't long before I drifted off to sleep. There were no dreams during this nap, just a dark void.

"Grace, Grace," I heard Drew's voice.

I wasn't sure where I was when I first woke up. I sat up and looked around. He crouched beside me.

"You okay, sleepy head?"

I took a deep breath.

"Tired."

"I know the feeling, Grace. I know the feeling."

He reached for my hand to help me stand up.

"Are you ready?" he asked.

"Yeah, I think so."

"Do you have the letter Jimmy left you?"

I had stuffed it into my pocket. I patted my pocket to make sure it was still there.

"I do."

He didn't let go of my hand as we walked from the dock to the car.

"I don't want you to trip and fall," he explained as he shined a flashlight on the path. Clouds now covered the once bright moon. It was much darker than before. I didn't feel like arguing as he led me back to his vehicle and opened the door for me to get in.

He waited until we'd gotten onto Washington Road, the main thoroughfare, before he said anything.

"Did you have a nice nap?" he asked.

"Not really. None of my naps this week have helped me catch up on sleep. They've just made things worse," I said with a brief laugh. "Did you find anything else?"

"No, I think I have enough."

"Who did this?"

"There will be a few tests run on the gun and the shirt – DNA, stuff like that, remember?" he commented.

"He shouldn't have died. I should've done something, Drew."

"Why do you keep beating yourself up? What else could you have done? He didn't confide in you that something was wrong before he died. He'd made up his mind," he said.

"I knew something was wrong, Drew."

"You did, but even though Jimmy Hughes had decided to take his own life, he didn't commit suicide. Someone else pulled that trigger, and if you'd followed him and tried to stop him, you might've ended up dead as well."

I didn't respond.

"There's enough evidence to arrest Debbie for theft or embezzlement. I don't know the exact charge. I don't know whether the gun and bloody shirt will connect her to the murder."

I started to ask him who he thought killed Jimmy, but he was already in tune with my line of thinking.

"Those items we found can't tell me who killed Jimmy until those tests are run. Whoever killed him knew about the garage at the lake, so that does narrow it down, but what happened tonight doesn't point me to the killer, Grace."

"I can't believe one of his family killed him."

"We don't know that for sure. You can't jump to conclusions. As far as I know, it could be Cal. We don't know. That's where the forensics come in. After you left, there was a team that came in to collect evidence."

"Drew, what time is it?"

He laughed.

"How you fell asleep on that dock is beyond me. You must really be exhausted to have done that, but you were out for a couple of hours. It's about 3:30. If we'd stayed longer, we could've watched the sunrise."

"Wow. I thought you said you were almost finished when I walked out to the dock."

"I was, but you were sleeping pretty peacefully, and I didn't want to wake you. Even though it didn't look too comfortable."

"Now that you mention it, I am a little sore."

I yawned. I was still tired.

"You're going to let me know how this ends, right? You aren't going to let me find out through the newspaper or radio, are you?"

"I've already told you I would, and I promise to let you know," he said softly.

It wasn't long after that that we arrived at the apartment.

"Let me walk you upstairs," he said. It wasn't a question.

After I unlocked the door and started to head into the apartment, Drew stopped me.

"Grace, would you have breakfast with me in the morning?"

It came from out of the blue, and without thinking, I said "yes," only to regret it as soon as I walked inside and locked the door behind me.

I was too tired to call him and get out of it. I collapsed into my bed.

13

I'd just fallen asleep when my alarm went off. I looked at my phone. I'd ignored it the night before. There were multiple missed messages, plus there was one from Drew, asking if 7 was too early. It was 6, so 7 would be fine. I texted him to meet me at my shop, and we could walk over to Buona Caffe.

As I took a quick shower, I remembered the letter Jimmy had written. I threw on a pair of white jeans and a printed top and sat down at my table to read the letter. I opened it and there were three pieces of paper in the envelope. A letter was folded separately from the two other sheets. I opened the letter first without opening the other pieces.

It started with the familiar "Little Lady" greeting.

Thank you for following up on all my clues. I'm sorry to have taped those papers under your desk, but I found them in Debbie's computer after I'd already taken everything else to the lake. She was trying to get rid of the evidence. I never laundered money, but I did almost make the mistake of borrowing money to take care of Jake's gambling debts. You should have enough evidence to lock Debbie away for a long time, and maybe even enough to put some of those J&M people behind bars. Steve Mathis is one of them. He's no good, and Peggy is blind, deaf, and dumb where he's concerned. What hurts the most in all of this is the betrayal by people I thought who cared about me. You were one of the few people who never did that. I hope that you will find happiness with Trevor Blake

143

one day. You've always been kind to me, and it wasn't because I was your customer. That's just who you are, Grace. You're good and kind. I want to give you something. Peggy and my kids don't care about my lake property except for the money it could bring them. They don't appreciate its beauty; they don't appreciate nature. You're different. I know how much you love that sort of thing. I have the acreage, the house that Cal lives in, and a small cottage. I want to give you the property. I hope that you'll make concessions for Cal and maybe move him to the other small cabin on the lake. It would be a better fit for him; he's a good guy. I've updated my will, too, but you'll find some important documents enclosed. I put the property in a trust, so my wishes will be followed. Some of my family never cared about what I wanted in life. In death, they have no choice.

I stared at the letter with tears streaming down my cheeks. I looked at the other pieces of paper – one was a property deed for the lake and the other was the title to the Camaro.

After a few moments, I wiped the tears away. I put on my makeup despite the humidity and the tears. I wasn't sure how long it would last on my face. I needed to cover up some of the dark circles and the puffiness. I was tired and emotionally drained, and I wasn't sure I was up to seeing Drew. But this was the morning I needed to tell him how I felt about everything.

I thought about texting Trevor, but he said he'd call me. I was sure he didn't want to know about my trip to the lake or the fact that I was having breakfast with Drew. What a day this would be. I guess it was appropriate given the week I'd already had.

I grabbed my funeral dress so I could change into it later. I wasn't wearing it all day. I got to my shop well before 7. I needed to make sure everything was in place for the weddings later in the day. Jazzy would be in to help Emmie. I was leaving early to prepare for Trevor's evening. I left the door open so Drew could come in.

He was early, but he'd showered and changed since he dropped me off in the wee hours of the morning.

"Did you get any sleep?" he asked when he came in.

"An hour, maybe."

144

"Buona. It's been a while since I went there."

"Yeah. After last night, I could use some strong tea this morning and lots of sugar."

Drew smiled.

"Those pastries Pat makes have lots of sugar, but they are so good. I've missed them."

We walked to Buona Caffe, a specialty coffee house located in a building that had seen many lives. It started off as a residence and was even a florist at one time. Not only did they serve various types of coffees, but they made tasty extras such as pastries and breakfast sandwiches. They also have another location in town with a roastery supplying other restaurants with their special brews.

"Good morning, Pat," I said as I walked in.

"Hi, Grace. Hi, Drew. Long time, no see," she said to him.

Pat and John were the owners. Pat was the genius behind the amazing pastries including her Morning Glory Muffin and dark chocolate orange scones. The Morning Glory muffins were made with grated carrots, crushed pineapple, raisins, and pecans and topped with raw sugar. Totally divine.

They'd taught me a few things about coffee, and even gave me a coffee tasting. Despite their best efforts, I still wasn't sold on coffee.

"I've missed your muffins and coffee," he said.

"One muffin, and how do you want your coffee?" she asked.

"I'll take a latte actually."

"Any flavors?"

"No, and I need the largest size you've got," he said with a laugh.

"You – a latte?" I asked and smiled.

"I've been experimenting with lots of different kinds of coffee. I've used it to replace alcohol," he said matter-of-factly.

I ordered the Morning Glory muffin and some sweet tea.

We found a quiet table in the midst of the other customers who were drinking coffee while staring at their laptops.

"You've been crying again," he said.

I looked away.

"I read Jimmy's letter this morning."

"Ah," was all he said.

I'd put it in my purse before I left. I knew he'd need to see it. I slipped it across the table, and I watched as he read it.

"I understand why you're crying," he said softly.

"Yeah," I said. "Drew, did you find anything out about the items you found last night?"

He laughed.

"You don't have much patience, do you? I haven't slept yet. Forensic tests and identification take a while," he said.

"I know. I just want to know what happened."

"I do, too. You'll be hearing about Debbie's arrest soon."

I took a bite of the muffin. It was indeed glorious.

"Jimmy seems to think you and Trevor will be getting married."

"A lot of people do."

"Could I ask you something, Grace?"

I braced myself for what might come next. Over the last few days, I'd relaxed around Drew. It hadn't been as uncomfortable as it had been in recent months.

"I guess it depends on what it is."

"I was wondering about you and Trevor."

"So are a lot of people," I shot back.

"I mean. You two still aren't dating?"

"No," I said trying to drag out the one syllable word for all it had. "What part of 'no' don't people understand?"

He furrowed his brow and glanced down, staring into his cup. He started talking without looking at me.

"Jimmy Hughes was right," he jerked his gaze from his cup to my face. "Divorcing you was the dumbest thing I've ever done in my entire life."

My mouth dropped. I wasn't sure why. This shouldn't have been a surprise. With everything Beth and Emmie had said, I knew this was coming. I thought I'd been expecting it. After all, I was going to set the record straight today. I was going to tell him how I felt, right?

"I never should've left you. I kick myself every day," he continued. His voice was soft and tender, but it cut into that damaged place in my heart. I'd felt this before. I'd heard similar words before. A year ago, we were in a similar situation.

I hadn't felt uncomfortable around him until now. I'd wanted to hear him say those things. I'd wanted him to tell me he wanted me back. Even though I loved Trevor, I still longed for what was familiar to me and what I could no longer have. But now that he was saying them, I realized I didn't want to hear him say those words after all. I took a deep breath. He was waiting for me to say something.

"Drew, the last time you and I sat together in a diner, you got to say what you wanted. Now, it's my turn," I tried to remain calm. I wanted him to listen to my words not my emotions.

"Okay."

"I've had a lot of time to think over the past several months. I lie in bed at night – alone – and one phrase rolls over in my brain," I said. "When you left me, you told me that we weren't working."

"Yeah, I did," he said.

"You were right. We weren't working, and the reason we weren't is both of us were broken. Broken people don't work, and in our brokenness, we couldn't work together. You were broken because you watched your best friend gun down his wife then kill himself. I was broken by the shattered dream of becoming a mom; the miscarriages and infertility broke me, but so did not being able to fix you, save you, save us. Being kidnapped, seeing dead bodies, watching a woman get killed as she pointed a gun to my head didn't help my brokenness."

I paused and looked at him. His gaze locked with mine.

"The bad thing about it was that I could see you were broken, but I couldn't see that I was, too. I thought I was fine until Zack and Trevor and Emmie and Beth and so many people pointed it out to me."

I took a sip of tea.

"Over the past few months, I've done a lot of soul searching. I said that I didn't want a relationship with Trevor because I didn't want to get hurt, but I think what I really meant was I didn't want to hurt him. All of my sharp, broken edges could slice through him. There have been a couple of times that I've reacted to him, and I know I've hurt him even though I didn't mean to. I didn't want to keep doing it. He appreciated that. He told me to heal."

I paused to watch Drew's face fall. I was tired of all the pain. I didn't want to go through it again, but I had to end it. I had to end it now.

"Since you left, I've learned a lot about myself – not just how broken I was or still am. I learned I can take care of myself. I learned I'm stronger than I thought. I learned that life still goes on and there's a lot of living still left to do. I have talked to a counselor. I have sucky health insurance, and it doesn't cover mental health. It's been expensive, so I haven't gone as much as I should. Seeing a therapist isn't the only path to mental health. There are other types of therapy – ice cream therapy with Emmie, working in Trevor's mom's rose garden and trying to bring it back to life, spending time with friends, praying, and taking walks. I'm starting to feel like a person again. I'm starting to feel alive again."

He nodded at me and took a sip of his coffee.

"I never thought I'd say this, Drew," I paused because I really couldn't believe I was actually going to say what was going through my mind. "But thank you. I never would've left you. I never would've ended our marriage. But it wasn't getting fixed. It wasn't working, and we were leaving it to die. I would've done anything to fix it, and maybe if we'd gone to counseling together, I might've seen my problems clearer. I was even willing to do that after the divorce was final in December. I will always love you, Drew. I'm not the same person though. I can't go back to the way things were."

I glanced around the café. I knew I wasn't finished, and

he was letting me talk. There was a freedom in being able to say everything that had been on my chest for months.

"You asked about Trevor. Here goes," I said and let out a deep breath. "Trevor and I aren't in a romantic relationship. We see each other several times a week, but I don't let him pay for my dinners out unless I can pay for his on another occasion. I pay for my concert and theater tickets. I'm a big girl, and I'll take care of myself. He doesn't know that I can't afford the therapist, but that's why there are doctor-patient confidentiality laws. I won't let him pay for my medical treatment."

Drew stared at me without interrupting.

"Trevor is kind. He makes me laugh. He listens to me when I talk. He values my opinion."

I stopped and looked at the uneaten muffin before continuing.

"And for your burning question," I started then paused. I was going to tell him things I hadn't even told Trevor yet. My voice was getting hoarse. "Yes, I am in love with him. There were still feelings left over from the first time I dated him. And if he asked me to marry him today, I'd say 'yes.'"

Drew grimaced.

"But Trevor doesn't talk with me about marriage or the future," I said. I could feel the tears stinging in my eyes. I didn't need Drew to see me crying yet again. I swallowed hard. "We even had a fight last night about me helping you on this case. He doesn't like it. He says I'm spying. I'm supposed to go to this big shindig for him and his new job tonight. His brothers want to celebrate, and he wasn't sure I still wanted to go. You probably won't see a ring on this finger for quite a while."

His face softened as he looked at me.

"Thank you, Grace," he said. "Thank you for telling me that."

"So, you are free to live your life, Drew Ward, but I can't be part of it."

I couldn't take it anymore. I got up and walked out of the

café, taking big, brisk steps to get back to my shop as quickly as I could. If it hadn't been for the shoes I was wearing, I probably would've broken into a jog. I didn't want Drew to see me cry, and I didn't want to cry anymore.

When I got back to the shop, Emmie was already there.

"Where have you been? I saw your -" she stopped midsentence. "What is going on?"

"Drew showed up. We had breakfast. I don't want to talk about this. Leave it alone because Drew will be here shortly."

I glared at her and headed into my office, where I sat down at my desk.

It wasn't long before I heard Drew talking to Emmie.

"She's in there," Emmie said.

I looked up to see Drew standing in the doorway.

"You left this," he said holding up Jimmy's letter and the property deed.

"Thank you. Is this really mine?"

"Looks that way. I guess we'll see how the money laundering turns out, and if anything gets held up in probate. I'm no lawyer, but a trust is supposed to protect assets."

"I wonder if he stayed there."

"Not sure. I'll have to check that out."

"I wonder why Cal didn't say anything last night."

"I can't answer that, but I'm going to find out," he said then paused. "Grace, there's one more thing."

I stared at him. He paused and took a breath.

"You aren't going to like this," he said. "You can't go to Jimmy's funeral today."

"What are you talking about?"

He came into my office, closing the door behind him, and sat down.

"And you can't tell anyone about what happened last night."

"Why?"

"Because the last time you figured out who killed someone,

you went to that person's house and confronted them."

"She was leaving the country, Drew. Someone had to stop her."

His mouth dropped.

"Do you hear yourself, Grace? Maybe someone should have, but not you. You've developed this new habit of confronting people, and it's a good thing in the right circumstance. Until I have definitive proof of what the evidence points to, you don't need to be around those people," he said.

He stood up and walked to the door.

"No funeral," he said as he opened the door. He nearly ran into Emmie as he walked out.

"What's going on?" Emmie asked.

Neither of us said anything.

"Do not tell anyone what happened last night," he said.

Emmie folded her arms against her chest and raised her eyebrows.

"This must be good," she interjected.

"She's not allowed to go to Jimmy's funeral. Do you understand that, Emmie?" he asked angrily.

"What am I supposed to tell my mother?" I asked.

"You'll think of something," he replied in monotone.

"I can't lie to her."

"Then, get Emmie to come up with an excuse."

"Thanks a lot, Drew," Emmie said.

"You've got a much better poker face and voice than Grace does, and you know it, Emmie," he said.

"Maybe so, but why can't she go to the funeral or tell me about last night?"

Drew scowled at her in response without saying a word as Emmie's eyes darted back and forth between the two of us in confusion. He turned his attention back to me.

"There will be several deputies at the funeral, and if they see you there, they will arrest you, Grace Ward. Am I making myself clear? Do you understand?"

"You're loud and clear, but no, I don't understand."

"You aren't going to obstruct my case. When I have answers, I'll let you know, but I don't need you making a scene. Stay here and make up something to tell Lottie. Peggy won't know you're missing," he said as he left my office.

I didn't say anything as he left. I was shaking, and I think there were still a few stray tears. I stared in front of me. He didn't say anything to Emmie on the way out. The bell rang as he left the shop. I glanced at the papers on my desk. I didn't know what I was supposed to do with Jimmy's property. As I thought about the possibilities, I was aware of Emmie standing at the door to my office. She was waiting for me to say something to her.

"Drew and I had our talk at breakfast this morning," I said without looking at her.

She came into my office and sat at my desk.

"Sounds like you had more than breakfast with him."

"Yeah, but I can't tell you about it. I don't want to get arrested."

I glanced up to see her wrinkle her nose.

"Oh sweetie, I think I know more about whatever happened than you give me credit for," she said. "Obviously, something happened to clue you in on who the killer was, and the killer will be at the funeral."

I shrugged my shoulders.

"That's what I thought," she said.

"I didn't say anything."

"Please, Grace, I'm observant; I can read between the lines; and I know you and Drew sometimes better than you know yourselves."

I tried to smile.

"True, Emmie."

"Never mind, even though I'm dying to find out who you narrowed it down to and how. Tell me about your breakfast with him instead."

I took a deep breath.

"He started to tell me that Jimmy was right and that he had made the biggest mistake of his life in divorcing me, but I wouldn't let him say anymore. I told him that he was right when he said we weren't working, and I actually thanked him for putting us both out of our misery."

Emmie's mouth dropped, and then it transformed into the biggest grin I'd ever seen.

"I'm proud of you, sweetie!"

"He asked me about Trevor, and I told him we were friends, that I was healing," I paused. "I also told him that if Trevor asked me to marry him today, I'd say 'yes.'"

She jumped out of the chair and gave me a hug.

"This is huge!" she exclaimed.

I shook my head.

"Trevor and I had a fight last night. He was upset that I was helping Drew. I can't tell him about what happened after he left last night, which is good because that would probably make him even more upset."

"Well, Drew has told you to butt out of the case now. Are you going to listen to him?"

"I don't think I have much choice. He's never threatened to send me to jail before."

"Then don't worry about it, sweetie. Besides, last time I checked, you have a big to-do tonight, and we've got weddings. It is June, you know; those June brides are counting on us. And you're ditching me to get your hair done."

I laughed.

"Beth is helping me. What am I going to tell my mother? You know I'll get the third degree."

"Tell her what I just told you. You're ditching Jazzy and me, and we have June brides. You've gone to the funeral home; you've visited Peggy at home; and you couldn't break away. It's not a complete lie."

I sighed.

"You're right. It's not a complete lie."

"It's a Saturday. The weekends are always our busiest times. I know that Jimmy was a friend, but it's bride season. And brides keep us in business."

"Emmie, Jimmy…" I started to tell her about the property he left me.

"What?"

"I don't know if I'm supposed to say anything. I need to get flowers going. These arrangements aren't going to make themselves."

"No, sweetie, they aren't. What time is Jazzy supposed to be here?"

"I'm here. I'm not late yet," Jazzy said as she entered my office. "You ladies don't look like you're working to me."

She laughed as she hugged Emmie then me.

"I miss seeing you," I said to Jazzy.

"I know, Shug. I miss this place. I miss you ladies. I don't like working with sick people," she said.

I laughed.

"I hear you," I said. "I wouldn't have made a good nurse."

From there, the talk turned to the weddings of the day and what needed to be accomplished. Trevor sent me a text. A former patient of his from the clinic had had a heart attack, and he went to the hospital to visit him. He told me he wouldn't make the funeral. That was a relief because I didn't want to tell him Drew said I couldn't go.

14

As I worked on some of the flowers for the evening wedding, I thought about the night before. What I thought about the most were the notes Jimmy had written to me and the fact that he'd left me a piece of property. I wondered if he'd left anything for Emmie. I always thought he liked her more than he liked me. The more I thought about it, the more I realized that not attending Jimmy's funeral wasn't an option for me. I had to pay my last respects even if it cost me. I walked back to my office and stared at my funeral dress that I'd hung on the door. It was already hot and steamy, and it was an outside service. I knew what Drew had said, but obviously Jimmy thought highly of me. I hadn't realized it until the past few days. I kept watching the clock as it inched toward noon. We'd gotten a lot accomplished among the three of us. Despite Drew's warning, I knew what I had to do. Out of respect for Jimmy, and Jimmy alone, I was going to his funeral.

I ducked into my office and changed into my dress and pumps.

I walked out to find Jazzy and Emmie standing there waiting for me. Jazzy had her hands on her hips, and Emmie had her arms folded across her chest.

"What do you think you're doing?" Emmie quizzed me.

"I'm going to the funeral of a dear friend."

"What about what Drew said to you?"

"First off, Drew is not going to arrest me in front of my mother. He may take me aside and fuss at me, but there's no way he will arrest me. I can promise you that. And if he did arrest me, which he's not going to do, I'd be in jail, so I'd miss Trevor's party. There is a silver lining to all of it," I said with a smile. Emmie started to say something. I held up my hand. "Nope, I'm not through. Besides, if I just go to the funeral, and don't say anything to Peggy or the family or anyone else for that matter, then Drew will be fine even if he's watching me."

Emmie scowled at me.

"Are you sure you want to go alone?"

"Emmie, you and Jazzy need to stay here. Actually, one of you needs to head to Sacred Heart before too much longer. Those flowers need to be delivered."

"Sweetie, what happened last night with you and Drew?"

"That part I'm not saying yet, but I promise when I can, I will. Honestly, the more I think about it, the more upsetting it is. So, I'm going to do what I need to do."

I drove to Westover Memorial Park alone, trying to convince myself that it would be fine. He couldn't prevent me from going to a funeral. I drove around until I saw a hearse and a couple of green funeral tents. It didn't look like there were that many chairs under the tents. Fortunately, there was a cover of trees where the plot was. I parked and walked toward the crowd, but I kept my distance. There were no empty chairs; I'd gotten there too late for that. In fact, the service was just underway when I arrived. So, I moved back out of the way underneath a shady tree. But with the mercury topping the 90s, the shade provided little relief. I kept my eyes fixed on the pastor, even though I couldn't hear him. I watched Peggy, Jake, Becca, and Clint. Even from the distance I could see my mother frowning at me, probably because I was late.

As I stood there, I felt someone block my breeze, and I felt a wave of fear.

"Ms. Ward, what in the hell are you doing here?" Drew asked

in the scariest version of his authoritarian voice I'd ever heard. I didn't turn to look at him, but I extended my arms behind me.

"Go ahead and arrest me." I said softly.

He pushed my hands back to my side.

"I'm not going to arrest you in front of your mother," he said, and I giggled to myself.

"Why are you here?"

He moved around to my side, where I could see his face. He had a steely gaze and his jaw was taut.

"Look, Drew. The past few days have made me realize that Jimmy cared about me far more than I knew. I had to come and pay my respects to him. I'm far enough away from the family so I won't cause a ruckus. I just wanted to say goodbye to him. I'll leave now if that makes you happy, but I needed to come."

"What if I stand here with you? Would you mind?' he seemed sincere.

"No, I don't mind. As soon as people start moving around, I'll go. I promise. I don't want to be seen anyway."

The funeral wasn't long. There was a song and a eulogy, and then people began to move from their chairs to form a line to hug Peggy, Jake, and Becca.

"I'll go before Mama stops me."

He gave me a faint smile.

"Thank you for not arresting me, Drew," I said as I started to walk briskly toward my car. I could explain to Mama later that I needed to get back to the flowers for the weekend's weddings.

But before I could get to my car, I heard Peggy calling my name. I turned to see her approaching me in the distance. Drew also looked on.

"I have to get back to the shop," I said and turned to walk again.

"No. I need to talk to you," she shouted.

Drew was between both of us, and he started making his way toward me. Peggy seemed to be barreling toward me like a bull after the red cape of a matador. I started to think that maybe I should've stayed away like Drew had suggested. Drew stopped and stood next to me as Peggy approached.

"Just what do you think you're doing here?" she growled at me.

I was stunned. I didn't know what to say, and I surely didn't know what she was so upset about. The last time I saw her she was happy to see me, or so I thought.

"Answer me," she demanded. Becca and Jake had jogged up behind her.

"I just came to say 'goodbye.' And I'm going back to the shop."

"I want to know what was going on between you and my husband."

Now, she'd lost me.

"Peggy, calm down," Drew said in his deep, scary voice.

"Calm down. Calm down. Just who do you think you are, Drew Ward, to be telling me to calm down? Get out of my way. I guess I know why the two of you split up."

Those words punched me in the stomach. She thought I was having an affair with Jimmy. How could she think that of me? I glanced at Drew, who moved between Peggy and me. His jaw was set. It was tighter than it had been.

"Peggy Hughes, don't you dare make accusations regarding Grace that you can't substantiate," Drew's voice bit into me even though his anger was directed at her now and not me. "You know that's not true."

I still couldn't breathe.

"Mama, stop it. What's gotten into you?" Becca tried to intervene.

"I got a call from my lawyer this morning. Jimmy apparently had a piece of property at the lake that I knew nothing about. But I found out this morning that Jimmy left it to her. He put it in a trust so I can't get to it."

Drew had moved in front of me to block Peggy, but I could see the stunned looks on the faces of Jake, Becca, and Clint when she said "lake." And I felt the blood drain out of my face as the accusations against me continued.

"See. I knew it. You knew about this property, didn't you? Did you go there with him?" she continued.

"Mama, stop it," Jake said. "Just stop it now."

"I will not."

"Peggy -"

I started to say something, but she wouldn't let me.

"I trusted you, Grace Ward. I let you into my home," she started to cry. Everyone was staring. Now we had the scene that Drew was trying to avoid.

"Peggy Hughes, you'd better think twice before accusing my daughter of something, especially when you know it's an absolute lie," Daddy intervened on that note.

"You stay out of this. Why did he leave her a house and land if there wasn't something going on between them?"

My mother pushed through and stood inches away from Peggy.

"Maybe it was because she was nice to him and listened to him," Mama interjected. "She took time to make all those flowers for you, entertaining every whim that came your way. I'll have you know she was arranging to get dahlias and hibiscus for your upcoming birthday. She got those crazy orchids when the ballerina was here, and all sorts of other ridiculous orders over the years. Do you know what she had to go through to get blue roses for your birthday a couple of years ago? They don't grow in that color."

My mother's voice was shrill. Peggy had ticked off the wrong person. It was bad enough that Drew was angry, but now she'd made Mama mad. Peggy had forgotten about me. I thought she was about to get into a knock-down, drag-out fight with my Mama right here in the cemetery. Drew stepped between Peggy and Mama. Peggy's mouth had dropped as she stared ahead of her. She glanced from

Mama to Drew to me and repeated the sequence.

"Stop it, all of you," Drew shouted. "That's enough. I'll arrest you all for disturbing the peace. Knock it off."

There was immediate silence as everyone stared at Drew. He turned his attention away and zoned in on Becca. Becca? I was confused. Why was he looking at Becca? I glanced at Jake and then back at Becca, and I noticed that everyone else was looking at Becca, too.

"Becca, what do you know about your dad's lake house and his garage?" Drew asked.

Both Becca's and Clint's faces were pale, but Jake's was bright red. He was angry.

"Nothing, Drew. I don't know what you're talking about," Becca said.

"I think you and I need to have a chat," Drew continued calmly.

Becca's eyes darted to her mother, boyfriend, and then to her brother and back to Drew.

"No, sir, Drew. I don't think we do."

"Drew Ward, this is my husband's funeral, and you have no right to question any of us," Peggy said.

"Becca, don't say anything until you get a lawyer," Clint said.

I didn't say anything, but something didn't feel right about the whole situation, and it wasn't just her accusations against me.

"That's fine, Peggy. Becca, do you want to come willingly with me now, or do I need to put you in handcuffs and take you in?"

"Drew Ward -" Peggy started angrily.

"Mama, enough. Just stop. Everyone just stop it, please," Becca said as she raised her hands and covered her ears. "I can't take all the fighting anymore."

She looked at Peggy and tears started forming in her eyes.

"Mama, Drew knows, and I think Grace does, too," she said.

Peggy stood and stared at Becca

"What does he know, Becca?"

"He knows that I – that I killed Daddy," Becca said as her voice cracked and she started to cry. She glanced back at Jake and Clint.

"Stop it, Becca," Jake interjected. "Listen to Clint. Don't say anything without a lawyer."

Drew and I were the only two people who weren't surprised by that bombshell. Okay. Maybe Drew wasn't the only one surprised by the bombshell. I was a little surprised by the confession, and I still couldn't shake the feeling that something was off with the whole situation. I glanced at my mother, who I thought might faint in the 95-degree heat, and I was pretty sure that Peggy was on her way to passing out as well.

"What did you do, Becca?" Peggy whispered. Her demeanor had radically changed. She had forgotten I was even there.

"I didn't mean to do it, Mama. I didn't. It was an accident. I went to see him the other night. He called me, and he sounded upset, angry. He told me he was going to pay off Jake's debts, but not the way anyone thought. He said he wasn't going to do the dirty work for someone else. He said there was quite a bit of insurance money, and that all of us would be taken care of."

Becca started to cry.

I looked at her, knowing that she was grasping at straws. None of what she was saying was true. He never mentioned the insurance to me, not that the insurance would've paid in the event of a suicide anyway. I glanced at Clint and Jake. Neither of them had any expression. They were both sweating, but then again, we all were.

"I kept him on the phone and drove to his shop. He planned to kill himself, Mama. When I got there, he had the gun. You know the one he bought that made you so angry. I tried to talk to him. I tried to convince him not to go through with it. He was upset that Debbie had stolen a bunch of money. He knew that she'd pissed off a lot of people, and they were coming after him. I tried to convince him not to kill himself. He cried. He kept telling me how much he loved you. We wrestled. I tried to take the gun away from him, and it

161

went off. There was blood everywhere," she said.

Another lie. If they'd struggled, the gun wouldn't have hit him squarely in the back of the head.

Peggy grabbed Becca and held her while both of them cried. Jake didn't say anything. He glared at Drew. He was still angry; he didn't cry or show any other emotion except anger. Clint just stood there. He was shocked and had turned deathly pale.

Mama came over to me and hugged me while Drew put his handcuffs on Becca. Peggy didn't say anything, but she followed Drew and Becca as long as she could.

"Did you know about this, Grace?" Mama asked me as she held me. I cried. I was so tired of crying.

Daddy came and hugged both of us. I pulled away after a few moments. I needed that hug.

"Yes, Jimmy had left me notes and sent me something in the mail. Sarah didn't give it to me until last night. It was a key and directions to the lake house Peggy was talking about. There was a title to a 1968 Camaro and a deed to the lake property that he left for me. While we were there, Drew found a gun and a bloody shirt. I guess Jake and Becca didn't know Jimmy had left me the house or she wouldn't have stored those things there. I don't know why she didn't dump them somewhere or throw them in the lake."

"Wow. That's incredible that he left you that. He always thought highly of you, Grace," Mama said.

"Yes, he did, Grace," Daddy echoed. "He said you'd grown into a fine woman and we should be proud of you. And we are."

I smiled through my tears.

I hugged them both.

"Listen, I need to get back to the shop. I've got weddings and Trevor's party tonight."

"Are you going to be okay, Gracie?" Daddy asked.

"I'll be fine. I'm glad I take Sundays off. I'm going to need a rest. Say a prayer for me because tonight is Trevor's family's party, and I'm not sure I'm up for it."

I might've said I was fine, but my hands were shaking.

"Of course, honey. You'll be fine," Daddy said.

I headed back to the shop. When I pulled into the parking lot, I sat there for a few minutes because I didn't remember making the drive. Lack of sleep, a confrontation with Drew, a confrontation with Peggy, and the confession by Becca left me stunned and drained. I knew something was off with the arrest. Something just didn't feel right. I looked at my phone. It was almost 2:30. It was a short funeral, but I was running out of time.

I walked in to see Emmie finishing some wedding bouquets.

"Well I'm glad to see you didn't get arrested," she said and laughed. I stared at her and laughed.

"Came pretty close."

Emmie tilted her head.

"Really?"

"No, he wasn't going to, but to say that he wasn't happy to see me was more than an understatement."

I sat down on the stool and leaned my elbows on the worktable. I realized how exhausted I was.

"Why are you here?" Emmie asked. "We have it all under control."

"Where's Jazzy?"

"Fleming wedding. She should be back soon."

"Ah."

Emmie had been making some bows when I came in, but she put the bright pink satin ribbon down and stared at me.

"What's wrong, sweetie?" she asked me.

"I'd tried to avoid being seen. I hid behind a tree. I didn't want to cause a ruckus. I just wanted to say 'goodbye,' but Peggy accused me of having an affair with Jimmy, and Drew arrested Becca," I rambled.

Emmie held up her hands and walked over to me.

"Whoa there, sweetie. Slow down. Say that one more time and go just a little slower. You need to fill in some of the back story."

"Why would you kill your father?" I asked as the realization started to sink in. Had Jimmy thought of me as a daughter? What had I done to make him feel that way? My heart ached.

"Grace."

I stood back up. I needed to do something. I grabbed a roll of ribbon and started making bows.

"Jimmy sent me a letter in the mail. I guess he mailed it the night he died," I started. Emmie took some of the ribbon and followed my lead all the while listening to the story of my previous 18 hours with her mouth dropped.

"Wow," she said and stared at me when I finished my story. "He left you property at the lake and a car?"

"Yeah, he did. And I don't know why."

Emmie put her hand on my arm as I continued to ramble.

"So, now you know why Drew didn't want me to tell you anything earlier. But I guess that doesn't matter since he's arrested someone. Just don't tell anyone else. I don't know if I'm still not supposed to tell or not."

"I'll wait until I see it on the news to talk about it. Okay?" she asked as she went back to the task of making bows.

As I stood there, Jazzy came in. She fanned herself with her hands.

"It's so hot out there that hens are laying hard-boiled eggs," she said.

Emmie and I laughed.

"You aren't joking. Wearing black at high noon in the sun baked my brain," I said.

"Don't you need to leave and get ready for tonight?" Emmie prompted.

"Do I have to?"

"Grace, have you talked to Trevor today?"

"No, he had to go see a patient. I haven't talked to him, but he didn't leave my apartment last night happy."

"What happened?"

"He and I had a disagreement last night, and I'm not sure he wants me to go with him. He told me I didn't have to go."

I bit my lip, and Emmie came over to give me a hug.

"Sounds like someone has had a rough night and day."

"You have no idea, Emmie," I said as she let me go. There were a few stray tears – Jimmy, Peggy's accusations, Drew, Trevor. It was all getting to me.

"Listen, sweetie, you need to go home, take a shower, and get all gussied up for tonight," Emmie said.

"I don't think I can handle it. I'm peopled out."

"Beth will be there. Trevor's the man of honor, so all eyes should be on him."

"I know, and I'm going for him although I don't even know if he's still mad at me or not."

"Everyone has misunderstandings. You and I have had some serious fights in our friendship, but we're still friends," she said in an attempt to comfort me.

"I know."

"Good. Now Jazzy and I have everything under control. You take care of you."

"Yes, ma'am, Miss Grace, we have all of this taken care of. I have done some of my best work," Jazzy interjected. "But I'd really like to come home with you and fix your hair and makeup for tonight."

I smiled.

"Jazzy, I'll take you up on that, just not tonight. Emmie would kill me."

"You got that right, Grace. Besides I thought Beth was coming over to help you."

"I am perfectly capable of dressing myself and putting on makeup," I said.

Emmie wrinkled her nose.

"You need a nap or food."

"Stop it."

"Yep, probably both."

"I'm going home, but I can't take a nap. And yes, Beth wants to try out some new makeup techniques on me. Yay," I said with zero enthusiasm. "I get to be a guinea pig. It must be my lucky day."

Emmie rolled her eyes at me.

"Have fun tonight. Okay? Don't sweat this," she said.

I nodded and headed back to my car. I was on autopilot for the drive back to my apartment. I wasn't inside long when I heard a knock on the door. I wasn't expecting anyone yet and slowly opened the door. It was Zack, and he didn't look too happy.

"Why was Drew Ward here yesterday?"

I folded my arms against my chest and stared at him.

"Hi, Zack; Hi, Grace. How are you, Zack? I'm great, Grace, and you?" I mocked him for his lack of social graces.

"I don't need empty chit chat with you. I need to know why Drew Ward came here and left with you and didn't return with you until 4 a.m. What's going on?"

"Wow, Zack. You aren't my dad."

"No, I'm your brother, and if Drew is weaseling his way back into your life, I will kill him, and then you and I will have some words."

"Whoa, there, Zack. You know that Jimmy Hughes was killed, right?"

He folded his arms against his chest.

"Oh yes, I've already heard how I missed the funeral."

I laughed.

"You missed more than that. Anyway, Sarah brought me an envelope from Jimmy last night. Apparently, it arrived a few days ago, but she was distracted. I've been, too. I haven't helped her out this week. What time did you get home, anyway?"

"It was about 9:30, and you weren't here. Mama helped Sarah this week. She's been fine. Where were you, Grace?"

"Zack, you do know that I'm almost 33 years old, right?"

"Doesn't make one bit of difference to me. You will always be my little sister, so that makes you 14 forever. You know what I told Drew if he ever hurt you again."

"It's not like that. I called Drew, and I asked him to come over," I said retelling the story for the umpteenth time. "I went with Drew – willingly. I knew I shouldn't go by myself. It led to a big breakthrough on his case. And he arrested Becca this morning."

"Becca?" Zack questioned. "Really?"

"Yes. It's sad."

"I never would've thought of her doing that."

"She confessed, but something just feels off about all of it. I can't put my finger on it," I sighed. "Look, Zack, Drew didn't do anything to hurt me, okay? He and I cleared the air of a lot of things this morning, and it was good. Then, he threatened to arrest me."

I laughed. I wanted to see if I could get a reaction out of Zack, and I did.

"What?" he gritted his teeth when he said that, and his hands curled into fists.

"Simmer down. He didn't want me going to Jimmy's funeral because of what happened last night. I guess it's understandable, but I felt like I owed it to Jimmy, especially when I found out he left me some property at the lake."

"What? Property at the lake," he asked.

"Yes, and a muscle car."

"Tell me more," Zack perked up.

I smiled.

"Drew was drooling over it. A Camaro. 1968, I think is what he said."

"Man, that is a nice car. What are you going to do with it?"

"I'm not sure, Zack. I need to make sure it's really mine first."

"Well, don't forget your protective and loving older brother," he laughed.

"I won't. Let's just see how this plays out first. Peggy was royally ticked off. She accused me of having an affair with Jimmy."

"What? That's so gross," he paused. Then a wicked grin passed across his face. "Do you want me to take care of Peggy for you?"

I punched him in the arm.

"No. Besides, Drew defended my honor. And you should've seen Mama. She put Peggy in her place. I haven't seen her in Mama Bear mode in a long time."

"I would've like to have seen that. I probably should've gone to the funeral, but this week was long, and the kids were super excited to see me. Sarah was too because that meant I could stay with the kids; she left around 9, and I haven't seen her since."

"She deserves time alone."

"Indeed," he agreed.

"One thing, Zack. If you're going to worry about Drew, then call or text him or something. I told him I was in love with Trevor and that if he proposed, I'd accept."

Zack's mouth dropped.

"Oh really? I thought you and Trevor were just friends," Zack sarcastically uttered those last two words.

I glanced down.

"We are, but I guess I'm holding out for things to change."

Zack pursed his lips and nodded.

"How did Drew take that?" he asked.

"Better than I expected."

"Thanks for the heads up. I'll check on him," he paused. "Is tonight Trevor's big party?"

"Yeah, it is."

"Are you okay, Grace?"

"I'm tired. I didn't sleep much last night, and everything is caving in on me. I'm exhausted, and Trevor and I had a disagreement last night."

"Let me guess. He doesn't like you helping Drew."

"Ding, ding, ding. And Zack wins that round!"

"Grace, I don't blame him. Drew has put you in some rough situations. I've already punched him once for you. I can do it again."

"That's not necessary. I know what happened. I've lived it,

and I don't need everyone reminding me about it. It's over now. We caught another bad guy or woman or whatever. I shouldn't see Drew anymore."

"As long as he stays sober," Zack countered.

I swallowed.

"I'm hoping he will."

"Me too, but he has a bad track record."

"Lived that, too," I reminded him. "Thanks for checking on me, but you don't need to go after Drew. It's all good."

"Glad to hear it. I'll see you later. Have fun tonight."

"Thanks."

I really just wanted to go to sleep. I knew I didn't have time for a nap. I sent Drew a text and told him I didn't feel right about Becca's confession. Something was off. He thanked me and said he felt that, too. He was glad to have his suspicions affirmed, and he'd let me know if anything else developed. As tired as I felt, it would be one of those naps that when you woke up, you couldn't remember your name or what year it was. I'd had too many of those in the past few days. I needed a long night's rest, but that would have to wait. The more pressing need was a shower. Standing outside on a hot and muggy June afternoon caused sweat to run down my body. I felt as gross as that sounded. I didn't have long after my shower before Beth showed up with a variety of makeup cases.

"What on earth is all of that?" I asked her.

"You and I both know this evening is important. You're going to turn heads."

"Tonight is about Trevor, not me. He and I are just friends."

"Yada, yada, yada. I've heard that line too many times. This party introduces Trevor to his brothers' colleagues and their significant others. It's like a debutante ball," she said.

"Thanks, Beth, like I didn't feel enough pressure."

"I'm sorry, honey. That's the reason he left Augusta in the first place. He didn't want to be in anyone's shadow; not his father's, not his brothers', and let's face it, you're the only reason he's staying here now."

"I know, Beth, and I want to support him. That's the reason I'm going with him to this thing, but I know this isn't what he wants to do with his life. He's still trying to please them for some reason I don't understand."

She smiled.

"And you, my dear Grace, need a confidence booster. You're seeing yourself as less than, and you shouldn't. You know that with the right makeup, the right hair, and the right dress you'll feel better about yourself. You need to ooze that confidence tonight. I remember the first time you wore makeup. It was lip gloss; remember that?"

I laughed.

"Yes, it smelled like cherries."

"And you were different when you wore it. You smiled more. You had this shimmer in your eyes. You need that same feeling tonight."

"You're not joking about that. I feel like I have no confidence at all," I said and plopped on the couch.

"What are you going to do with your hair?" she asked, ignoring my theatrics.

I shrugged.

"Why don't you do a loose bun?"

"Can you help me with that, too?"

She smiled.

"Of course. That's why I'm here."

"Beth, you know that Jazzy would rather be doing my hair and makeup than going to Augusta Tech for a medical certificate, right?"

"Yeah, I know that, and I'm going to have a talk with her."

"Good. Let's get this over with," I said as I moved to the kitchen table. "When are you getting ready?"

"Don't worry about me, Grace. It will be fine. Isn't Trevor coming early to get you?"

"Yes, he is."

"I'll be long gone by then, and I have plenty of time."

We talked about the events of the day, the trip to the lake, and the arrest in between Beth coaching me on how to apply her makeup. She didn't apply it herself, especially the eye makeup. She had much more of an inventory than I did. Beth bringing over her makeup took me back a few years, and it was more fun than I thought it would be. With her suggestions, I was surprised at the woman looking back at me in the mirror.

"You look amazing," she declared at the almost finished product. The only thing we hadn't applied was lipstick.

"Thanks, Beth. You know how to cheer a girl up."

"Well, I still don't get invited to yours and Emmie's sleepovers. She calls you her 'best friend,' but I've known you longer," she said with a fake pout.

I shrugged and laughed.

"I think it's safe to say that you, Emmie, and I are the three musketeers or three stooges or something."

She laughed.

"Agreed. We're something, all right," she said with a chuckle. She handed me a tube of lipstick.

"Wear that tonight. You can keep it," she said.

"A dress and now lipstick. It's not my birthday."

"Well, it's right around the corner. So, consider it an early present if you like."

"You should go and get ready. I need you there as early as you can get there."

"Just don't go outside before Trevor gets here. You don't need your face melting before then," she said, and we both laughed.

"It's not going to be much cooler when he arrives. There's still time for it to melt from here to the car and from the car to the country club door."

Beth laughed.

"Don't follow me to the door," she said. "I'll see you soon. You look fabulous; own it, Grace."

She gathered up all her makeup and gave me a hug. It was too soon to put on the dress, so I sat and tried to catch my breath. I tried not to think about everything that had transpired over the past few days. If I did, I knew I'd start crying, and I didn't have all the tools to touch up the makeup.

15

I must've dozed off while waiting for Trevor. I woke to the sound of someone knocking on my door. I panicked as I looked at my phone to see the time. I wasn't dressed. I hoped I hadn't smeared my makeup. I rushed to the door wearing the tank top and shorts I'd put on while we did my make-up

I opened the door to see Trevor holding a beautiful arrangement of flowers. My heart fluttered when I saw him in his tuxedo with his crisp white shirt and black bow tie. When he saw me, he smiled, but it quickly faded, probably because I wasn't ready.

"Come in," I said. "I'm almost ready. I just need to put on my dress and shoes."

He placed the arrangement on the table. A mix of my favorite blue larkspur (or by their fancy name delphinium elatum), pink peonies, and red roses, it had Emmie's signature all over it. There were sprigs with iridescent pearl-like bulbs on them interspersed among the flowers and the greenery. It was stunning.

"Emmie said that these peonies were left over from the McIntosh-Williamson bouquets," he said.

I laughed. I wondered if he'd told her to use the peonies. There was a lot of love put in that arrangement, and it wasn't just Emmie's. He was sending me a message. He knew I loved to research the meanings of flowers, and he often asked me what certain ones meant. Everyone knew that red roses symbolized love. The leftover peonies spoke of love at first sight. And the blue ones were my favorite, and he knew that. The pearls were a sweet touch.

"You didn't have to do that," I said.

"I never have to do anything. I wanted to, and there's this great little floral shop that I love to buy things from. They always know how to put a smile on someone's face," he said softly. I smiled.

"Emmie outdid herself."

"They were made with great love," he said.

"I'll go slip the dress on," I said, but he reached out and touched my wrist.

"Please wait," he said. "I wanted to apologize for last night."

"You don't have anything to apologize for. You have a right to your opinion," I said.

"I could've handled things better, and I know I hurt you when I told you that you didn't need to come tonight. I could see it in your eyes."

"It's okay, Trevor."

"No, it's not okay. I promised I'd never hurt you, and I did. I've felt awful about it. Apologizing over a text message or phone call isn't good enough. That's the reason I waited until now."

"Trevor, in any type of relationship worth having there's going to be times when you hurt someone and you don't mean to. I know I've hurt you without intending to. It's unavoidable. If it's intentional, that's a problem."

"You look beautiful, but you aren't dressed. Are you thinking about not going?"

"No, that's not it. I just fell asleep," I paused. I was going to have to tell my story yet again. "I spent most of the past 24 hours or so with Drew."

He took a breath and started to say something.

"It's not what you're thinking," I said as I spilled the story to him except for the part about me telling Drew I'd accept Trevor's proposal if he made one. Trevor listened to everything. By this time, I wished I'd recorded everything I'd said the first time, so I didn't have to keep repeating myself. "So, I've had little sleep, and I'm on edge from everything that's happened during the week, but Beth said she'd help me out."

He smiled.

"Let me put on the dress, and I'll be back out."

I changed in my tiny bathroom. The one thing I didn't have in my apartment that I wished I had was a full-length mirror. I walked out of the bathroom to see Trevor waiting.

"You look incredible," he said. "All eyes will be on you tonight."

"No, I'm not the guest of honor at this thing. All eyes should be on you."

"Why would anyone look at me when you're there?" he whispered the words as he stared at me.

I think I blushed with that remark. I hadn't blushed in a long time.

"Wow, you're smooth," I said and laughed. "But thank you."

I put on a pair of black, high-heeled sandals.

"Before we go, I need to tell you something," he said. "I may have overreacted about you helping Drew this time. I really thought about why it bothered me, and to be honest, I think I was jealous."

"Why would you be jealous?"

"Because when you're helping Drew on a case, you're focused. Your total attention is devoted to that, and it causes you to spend a lot of time with him – time you hadn't been spending with him. You start to act differently. You close yourself off from me, and I wonder if you're opening up more to him. So, I got jealous."

I reached out and touched his arm.

"I'm so sorry, Trevor. I didn't know that I did that," I said knowing I needed to tell him the rest of the story of last night. "I left out part of my story. Drew and I ended up spending most of last night together tracking down clues. This morning when he dropped me off at my apartment around 4, he asked me to breakfast. He told me that Jimmy was right when he'd said divorcing me was the dumbest thing he'd ever done. I stopped him, and I told him that while I still cared about him, there was no way I could get back with him. It wasn't happening. And I told him that he did us both a favor because our relationship was dying and neither of us were doing anything to resurrect it. I never would've been the one to leave. I'm almost glad now that he did."

A relieved look passed over Trevor's face. He touched my cheek.

"That makes me feel better," he said. "Are you ready to go now?"

"Absolutely."

"Grace, tonight. I don't know what tonight holds. All I know is that I'm nervous about it. I'm afraid one of my brothers is going to do something. I don't know what they're up to."

He looked at me as though he wanted to say something but wasn't sure he should.

"Could I have a kiss for luck?" he whispered.

The request surprised me, but I smiled as he stepped toward me, placing one hand on my waist. He touched my face and leaned in to kiss me.

"Why don't we just ditch everyone else tonight and spend the evening together?" he asked.

"Sounds good to me," I giggled.

"I wish I could. You don't know how much I wish that, Grace. You honestly don't know."

He took a deep breath, letting me go to walk toward the door.

"Did you ever find out how many people will be there tonight?" I asked once we'd gotten in the car.

"I have no idea. I'm almost afraid to ask at this point. It swelled from being just the family."

The soiree was at the country club. I'd only been to the country club once or twice in my life. Once was with Trevor's family when I was dating him as a teenager. I remember it being awkward, as I'm sure this would be. The country club has several meeting spaces.

Trevor is a stickler for being on time, and we arrived before most of the other guests and two of his brothers. Richard, Trevor's eldest brother, was already there and pounced on Trevor as soon as he saw him.

"Well, there's the man of honor now," Richard said as he reached out to shake Trevor's hand. Richard didn't even acknowledge my existence as he whisked Trevor away to talk to a couple of other early birds, and I glanced around for the nearest exit. I wondered if he'd notice if I slipped into the hallway and stayed there for the rest of the night. I wasn't sure about the plan for the evening. I thought there would be cocktails and a seated dinner. Maybe I could just return at a later time, like when it was time to eat. I started walking toward the door because I knew I'd feel much more comfortable in the hallway than in the room. I moved quickly and was relieved when I saw Beth and Knox in the hallway.

"You have no idea how glad I am to see you," I said.

"It can't be that bad already."

I took a deep breath.

"You look wonderful, Beth."

She looked perfect with her blonde hair swept up into a French twist. She wore the royal blue dress she'd told me about. It fit her form perfectly, showing off her figure, and she wore those fabulous stilettos she reserved for social functions.

"You don't look so shabby yourself, Grace. That dress looks perfect on you."

She smiled and leaned to whisper in my ear.

"Remember to flaunt it, but not too much," she said and giggled.

"I'll keep that in mind."

"Just stay with me and the other wives. You'll be fine. I'll protect you."

She was right. The gathering was segregated by gender. All the men seemed to be clumped on one side of the room with the women chatting on the other. They seemed to like it that way. I glanced at the tables; there were no name cards.

Dinner was scheduled after the cocktail hour, according to Beth, who knew more details than I did. I didn't receive a printed invitation, but apparently, there were some of those. I watched Trevor as he mingled. I'd catch his eye every so often, and he'd smile at me. Every time he headed my way, someone stopped him and started to talk to him.

"Grace, let's mingle, too," Beth suggested. "We can talk business. Most of these ladies know our designs, and some of them need our services."

I nodded as she introduced me to a couple of other women in the room.

"Grace, I need you to meet Marianna Spencer. Her daughter, Bethany, is getting married in the spring. I know you will be looking at floral designers. I work with Grace," she said, introducing me to one of the women nearby.

"Oh, yes. We're looking at flowers now. Planning a wedding is time-consuming. Bethany has strong ideas on what she wants. She doesn't want it to be too trendy. She said she wants a vintage look."

I smiled as I took a card out of my purse.

"We can do whatever you're looking for. I have a portfolio of designs, and we can create her own signature look. Don't hesitate to call us."

She took my card.

"I'll put you on the list. I've seen some of the things Beth has done. Her home always looks perfect."

From there, conversation turned to the weather, and my pedigree. Your parents and other forebears are important in the South. It seemed I was always running into someone who could be my third cousin, twice removed.

"Didn't I see you at Jimmy's funeral and at Jimmy and Peggy's house?" she asked.

"Yes, my parents are friends of theirs, and Jimmy is – was – my best customer."

"Peggy is my mother's first cousin. My grandfather and her mother were siblings."

"Small world," I said.

"And your mom is Lottie Burke. I love her lemon pound cake. I wanted to take a couple of pieces and hide them in my purse after I was at Peggy's, but I didn't. She should start her own bakery."

"She's been told that, but she doesn't want the hassle, although cakes and flowers would make a great business."

"You could corner the wedding market," Marianna said and laughed. "I can't believe I've never met you before today."

Marianna started to say something else, but she was distracted. I followed Marianna's eyes to the door as a woman walked into the room. I'd never seen her before. She was tall and slender and had straight dark brown, shoulder-length hair. She was attractive and had a presence about her – strong, confident. I noticed her chatting with a few people. Her face was animated, and I could see her eyes twinkle as she smiled. She hugged Trevor's sister-in-law, Claire, as though she was an old friend she hadn't seen in a long time. They smiled at each other and talked for a few moments. She followed suit with the other women in that klatch.

I turned to glance at Beth, whose face had gone pale. She moved closer to me and held my hand. I was confused. Beth's furrowed brow contradicted the smile she gave me. She patted my hand as my eyes darted back to Trevor who stood motionless and with a look of horror as the woman chatted with other people. When she noticed him staring at her, she walked straight toward him without pausing to talk with anyone else. I glanced back at Trevor. His mouth had dropped, and I saw him shaking his head "no." When the woman reached him, she linked her arms seductively around his neck. I took a deep breath as the unfamiliar pangs of jealousy hit me.

I turned back to Beth and started to move, but she wouldn't let go of my hand.

"Just wait," she mouthed.

Why was Beth trying to keep me in place? I stared at her for a moment. She shook her head "no" at me. I glanced back to Trevor and the woman. I wondered what she was whispering in his ear. He didn't embrace her despite the fact that she'd pressed her body close to his and still kept her arms around his neck. I felt my heart drop as I watched her. I wanted to leave. I didn't want to watch what was going on, but I couldn't tear my eyes away. He leaned in to whisper in her ear causing her to release him abruptly. He turned and glared at his brother, Richard, who stood nearby. Without looking at her and without saying anything to anyone, he began to walk toward me. He wasn't happy, and for a moment, I didn't see Trevor's face, but Drew's. He had a steely stare, and his jaw was clenched tightly as he reached for me. Beth let go of my hand as he placed his hand on my hip and leaned to whisper into my ear.

"Grace, we're leaving, but before we do, I'm going to kiss you; here in front of everyone, and I really hope you don't mind," he said, moving his hand to the small of my back and pulling me close to him.

His eyes locked with mine, and he smiled. He gently stroked my cheek before his lips touched mine. It wasn't just a peck either. It was a long, passionate kiss, and it took my breath away. I wasn't sure what the reason was, but I didn't care. As far as I was concerned, there was no one else in the room.

After he'd released me, he smiled and nodded at me, signifying he was ready to leave. I couldn't respond. I couldn't breathe. Trevor wasn't the alpha male type, and that move was totally out of his nature. He held my hand and led me out of the room. I knew everyone was staring at us, especially Beth. I tried not to look around, keeping my eyes fixed on him as we left. Still in my periphery, I couldn't help but notice a few people with their mouths agape as I passed them. And I did hear a couple of glasses shatter as they hit the floor.

He said nothing on the walk out of the country club to his car. He opened the door for me and walked around to the driver's side. His only words on the drive were, "I'll tell you everything shortly. Just give me a minute to breathe and gather my thoughts."

I could accept that especially as I watched him shake his head as though he was silently replaying what had just happened. He'd gritted his jaw as he focused on the road ahead of him. Obviously, I wondered who the woman was, and I wondered why her appearance made him so angry that he decided to leave before we ate before what was supposed to be an evening about him and his new job. I wondered what I was missing. I seemed to have been the only person in that room who didn't know who she was. From her actions, she seemed to have been romantically involved with him at one time, but he didn't respond to her, which made me feel better.

It was a short drive to his house. Without saying a word, he helped me out of the car and opened the front door. He took off his jacket and threw it on one of the chairs before heading to the back porch. That was totally out of character for someone who believed everything had its place.

Unsure what to do, I followed slowly. When Drew was angry about something, I walked on eggshells in a desperate attempt not to upset him anymore. I was afraid to say or do much. I didn't want to go down that path again, even though I knew Trevor wasn't angry with me.

I walked to the door and stepped outside. Trevor was leaning on the bannister, gazing into the distance. There was still plenty of daylight left so I could see him and his clenched jaw. He didn't look at me, and he didn't say anything. I wasn't about to break the silence. I turned to go back into the house. I was starting to get hungry, and I could pull something together. He always had plenty of fresh ingredients, plus I'd promised him some homemade salsa with the items from the garden I'd planted. The screen door squeaked as I opened it.

"Grace, please don't go," he said.

I stopped and turned back to see him still staring out into the distance.

"I'm just going to go into the kitchen to fix us something to eat. I'll leave you alone," I whispered.

He turned to look at me.

"It's one thing for my brother to meddle in my professional life; it's another for him to interfere in my personal life, in my love life. He crossed a line tonight," Trevor said with a clenched jaw. "He's always been like my father, and he's always tried to be a second father, and I don't mean that in a good way."

"I'm sorry, Trevor."

"What for? You've done nothing to be sorry for," he said. He walked toward me and opened the door so we could go back inside. I walked in and stepped back. I wasn't sure what he was going to do. He walked into the sunroom and I followed him. There, he sank into the overstuffed couch. I sat next to him as he stared off into the distance for a few moments.

"He kept introducing me to oncologists trying to get me to join a practice. He pushed me into applying for this job. He's always been there pushing me. And I could handle that. Tonight, though. Tonight was a different story."

He sucked in a deep breath.

"Listen, Trevor, if you don't want to talk about this, I can go fix us something to eat, and we can talk later," I said quietly.

Trevor looked at me.

"Why are you looking at me like that, Grace?"

"Like what?"

"Like you're afraid of me."

I hesitated. I wasn't sure what to say to him at first.

"When Drew was angry, it was best for me to stay quiet and out of his way," I whispered.

"I am not Drew, Grace," he said sharply, emphasizing each word.

"I know. I just don't know how to deal with anyone when they're angry, especially as angry as you are now."

He reached out for my hand.

"You know I'm not angry with you, don't you?"

"Of course, I do. But I've never seen you this way before. I don't know how to act. I know you aren't Drew, but he's the only one I've dealt with on a regular basis who got angry. When he did, it was best for me not to say anything; otherwise, there'd be a shouting match and possibly a broken coffee pot."

Trevor's expression softened slightly as he gently touched my cheek.

"I'm not Drew. I promise you. I'm not Drew. I would never take my anger out on you," he repeated in a soft whisper.

"I know."

He turned away from me and sucked in another deep breath as though he was trying to calm his nerves. He stood up and walked across the room. Then he turned back to glance at me again.

"Angry doesn't even begin to describe how I feel right now. I didn't mean to frighten you. We can eat later. I do want to talk about what happened because I don't want you walking on eggshells around me, ever. Okay?"

"Okay."

He gazed around the room as though he was still trying to gather his thoughts.

"Do you remember when I told you that I'd dated someone while I was in medical school?"

"Yes."

"Her name was Kennedy Harrison, and she was the woman who showed up tonight, invited by my brother, Richard."

Anger punctuated the final words of that sentence.

"Oh," I said slowly. "She's stunning."

He nodded. He walked back and sat down next to me.

"Stunning, yes. She's beautiful, brilliant, dedicated, and driven," he said maintaining his eye contact with me. That sick feeling returned. I felt inadequate next to someone like her. "I met Kennedy while taking a break from studying one night. We struck up a conversation. I asked her out for coffee, and we hit it off. Both of her parents are doctors. Her older sister and brother are doctors. We were both the babies in highly successful families and expected to follow in their footsteps. We had a lot in common, or so I thought. It wasn't long before we'd moved in together. My father adored her and so did Richard, who even talked with her about the possibility of her joining his practice one day. Those should've been my warning signs. Neither my father nor Richard was ever driven by anything except calculating logic. Neither of them had any emotions. Everyone loved Kennedy. She just had this way about her. Everybody except my mother, that is. Mama hated her. Well, hate is a strong word for Mama. Mama never hated anyone, but she didn't like Kennedy at all. I didn't find that out until right before she died, though. She said 'I'm so glad you didn't marry that Kennedy girl. She wasn't good for you.'"

I smiled.

"I could tell you weren't expecting her to show up tonight."

"Talk about the understatement of the year, Grace. I never thought I'd see her again. Kennedy had her life planned out. She had a five-year plan, a 10-year plan, 15- and 20 year-plans. She knew at what age she wanted to get married and have her two children – one boy and one girl. I think she even knew at what time and on what day she would die," he laughed sardonically. "I didn't find out some of those details until it was too late. At Christmas break, she and I went to New York together, and I proposed to her at Rockefeller Plaza. She said 'yes,' but whenever I'd try to talk dates or about our future, she'd change the subject. Then I found out she was considering applying for residencies on the other side of the country so, I asked her if she loved me. She said 'of course, silly' and laughed it off. Then I asked her if she was 'in love' with me. She looked confused and didn't answer right away. I asked her why she agreed to marry me. She said that we were compatible and that as a doctor, she'd need someone of equal social standing. She wanted her children to be intelligent, athletic, and highly successful. She needed a partner like me. She'd met my family and felt we had good genes. I read between her lines to see that she only wanted me because of my position. If I'd been a carpenter or a plumber, she never would've given me the time of day.

When I told you that no woman ever wanted me for me, I never lied. Kennedy wanted to marry a doctor or some other professional. Who that man was didn't really matter to her. She wanted someone with a pedigree, and I was the first that came along. I told her that it was over right then. She laughed. She didn't believe me. She went to class and told me she'd see me that night. My class was later than hers. I called a friend and asked if I could live on his couch for the rest of the year. He agreed, and I moved out. I didn't answer her phone calls. I told her I was done, and I meant it."

"Wow. I'm sorry, Trevor."

He smiled and shook his head "no" at me.

"Sorry for what, Grace? For me not making the biggest mistake of my life?"

I shrugged my shoulders weakly and tried to smile.

"When she hugged me tonight, she whispered that my brother had told her I wasn't seeing anyone, and she invited me for a drink at her hotel room after dinner."

He paused. He searched my face for a reaction. I glanced down. I didn't want him to see inside me.

"Well, it's not like you and I are seeing each other, Trevor. We're just friends." I had a hard time choking out those words.

He touched my chin and gently turned my face to his.

"Grace, stop. This is me you're talking to," he whispered it, but there was a sharp edge in his tone. "You keep saying we're 'just friends' to everyone, but this is me. If you don't feel anything for me except friendship, then maybe…"

He glanced away.

"Maybe?" my voice was breathy, and my heart started to ache.

"While the calendar may say it's only been nine months since Drew left you, it seems like we've been together much longer. To me, this has been one of those old-fashioned courtships, basing everything on a friendship, not a physical relationship. I've been fine with that, but now, I need to know if you only think of me as just a friend. After that kiss at the country club, it's going to be hard to convince anyone otherwise."

I smiled. He waited for me to say something.

"It *was* an amazing kiss," I agreed.

Trevor didn't respond. He was still waiting for me to say something else. It was uncomfortable. I didn't know what he wanted me to say. He kept staring at me in awkward silence for several moments.

He finally took a breath.

"So, Grace, are you and I just friends? Is that all you feel for me? Is that all I'll ever be to you – just a friend? If that's all this is to you, then maybe you and I shouldn't spend as much time together. Maybe I should do as Drew did, and let you live your own life."

He sounded so sad when he said those words that punched into my heart. I could feel the tears stinging in my eyes.

"Do you want me to tell you that Beth held my hand so I wouldn't make a scene? I think she was afraid I'd embarrass myself or you."

His face softened as a smile formed on his lips.

"That's a good start. But why would you have embarrassed yourself?" he asked and winked at me.

"Because I might've wanted to deck someone or storm out of the room. I'm really not sure which one I planned to do."

He tilted his head and smiled.

"Really? I never knew there was a violent streak in you, Grace," he said. "And what would possess you to start a cat fight in the country club dressed like that?"

I paused.

"Being jealous of that gorgeous, perfect woman who walked up to you and pressed her body against yours in front of everyone in the room."

"Jealous?" he asked with a playful grin.

I glanced away again.

"Of course, I was jealous. I'm -" I paused. I couldn't believe I was going to say what was in my brain. I looked into his eyes. "I'm madly, deeply, passionately, hopelessly, and utterly head-over-heels in love with you."

There. I'd finally said it. I'd been afraid to admit it. He smiled and reached out to touch my face.

"I love you, too, Grace."

"Well it's true. I am. I'm in love with an incredible man," I whispered. "And we have been 'just friends' all this time for a lot of reasons. I didn't want you to think I was only interested in you because you're a doctor or because of your money. I wanted you to know that I was interested in you."

"Oh, I knew that already, Grace, but it really would be nice for you to let me pay for your dinner and the plays and concerts we go to," he laughed.

I smiled.

"I'm an adult, and I can take care of myself."

"I know that, too, but I want to give you so many things," he paused and took a deep breath before a mischievous grin came across his face. "You're in love with me, Grace?"

"Yes. Very much."

"Hold that thought," he said as he got up and left the room for a few minutes. When he came back, he sat next to me and reached out for my hand. He looked into my eyes.

"I need a huge favor from you, Grace."

I was confused.

"Of course, Trevor. Anything you want."

"Anything?" he asked as he winked at me. I noticed a gleam in his eyes. I wasn't sure what he was talking about.

"Within reason. I won't rob a bank or kill anyone," I said and laughed.

"Nope. Not going to ask you to do either of those. I told Kennedy a lie, but you can make me an honest man."

"Okay?" I dragged those two syllables out slowly. I was asking a question; not making a statement.

He took a deep breath.

"This isn't how I imagined it," he said almost as though he was talking to himself.

"What are you talking about?"

"My lie is I told Kennedy that my brother was sorely mistaken when he said I wasn't seeing anyone. Not only was I seeing someone, but we're engaged and just haven't told our families yet."

I noticed he was holding a small velvet box in his hand. He slipped to one knee. I took a nervous deep breath as I felt tears brimming in my eyes. My hands seemed to instinctively cover my mouth as I gasped. This wasn't how I expected the evening to go. This week had ranked up there with one of the worse weeks of my life up to this point.

He opened the box, and I saw a beautiful ring. There was a pearl encircled by tiny diamonds. The band had small diamonds embedded in it.

"Grace, all those adverbs you said earlier – totally, madly, deeply, utterly," he smiled as he paused. "That sums up how I feel about you, too. Totally, utterly, madly, deeply, truly, and unashamedly head-over-heels in love with you. These past several months have been difficult with my mother dying and almost losing you at Christmas after I'd just found you again. I knew that I'd have to wait to do this for you to heal from Drew, but I knew I didn't want life without you ever again. And I don't know if you're ready for this. I don't think you're completely healed. I don't know if you're still in love with Drew…"

He paused as he stumbled over his words and looked at me for some type of sign that he was doing the right thing. The tears freely fell down my cheeks. It didn't matter to me that he didn't have some grand proposal at the top of the Empire State Building planned. All I wanted was this. I reached out to touch his cheek.

"Grace, will you marry me?"

"Yes." I whispered.

He took my left hand and slid the ring on my finger. It was the most beautiful ring I'd ever seen. He kissed my hand before sitting next to me on the couch.

"I've carried that ring with me for a couple of months now," he said. "When I went to Charlotte at Christmas to put my condo on the market, I met with a former patient who designs jewelry. My mother's favorite jewelry items were her strands of pearls. She told me she had a lot of reasons she loved pearls best. Pearls signify wisdom, and she always thought that was one of the most important things you could have. She also loved that parable about the man who found the precious pearl and sold everything he had to buy that. She related that to a lot of things – not a physical pearl, necessarily. She said she thought of that pearl as a relationship. When you have a relationship that means the world to you, you make sacrifices for it. And you, Grace, are my pearl of great price. Pearls are graceful, beautiful. I also have a couple of strands of pearls to give to you. My mother said every Southern woman needed a strand of pearls, and she hoped someday you'd wear her pearls at our wedding."

My heart fluttered when he said "wedding."

"I'd be honored to do that, and this ring – it's absolutely beautiful, Trevor."

"Not as beautiful as you," he leaned over to give me a kiss.

I couldn't believe this was happening, but I was so happy it was.

The door chime interrupted our kiss. He laughed.

"I'm surprised we were alone as long as we were," he said as he released me and started to stand up.

"What do you mean?"

"That has to be an angry brother or two at the door," he said. "That kiss plus my leaving before the party began caused quite a commotion, don't you think?"

He walked to the door. I wasn't sure whether to follow or stay put so I followed at a distance. Trevor opened the door, and he was right. His brother, Edward, was at the door.

"Trevor, we've come to apologize," Edward said.

Trevor folded his arms against his chest and stood in the

doorway. I could see Edward's wife, Vivian, next to him and his brother, James, and his wife, Claire, at the door as well.

"Trevor, can we come in?" James asked.

Trevor didn't move for several seconds, but he reluctantly stepped back, allowing them in. The two women spotted me and smiled, making a beeline for me and my ring. Claire was short with short dark hair; and she had great decorating sense. Vivian was blonde and statuesque and always perfectly coiffed, dressed, and manicured. Vivian used that fashion-sense for financial gain and owned a small boutique. She was probably my favorite of the sisters-in-law. The two women came toward me and gave me hugs, and then they wanted to see the ring, which they gushed over.

"Please believe us when we say we had no idea that Richard was going to pull that stunt and make your night all about him," Edward continued.

"And believe us when we say we were just as blindsided by Kennedy's appearance as you were," James added.

Trevor didn't say anything. He was still angry at them.

"We also wanted to tell you that we're proud of you," Edward said.

Trevor folded his arms against his chest.

"Oh really? So glad I have your approval," his voice dripped with biting sarcasm.

James put his arm around Trevor.

"Yes, we haven't treated you fairly. I think we all still think of you as our baby brother, and that's wrong," he said.

"And we're proud of you for standing up to Richard," Edward said.

"He had no right to do that," Trevor growled.

"You're right, Trevor. He crossed a line," Edward paused and smiled. "You should've seen his face when you kissed Grace."

"What a kiss! I think the temperature went up about 15 degrees in the room," Vivian started fanning herself as she said that. She glanced at me and winked. I could feel my cheeks burning. "I'm surprised Grace didn't melt right there. I thought I was going to. Eddie, you should kiss me like that sometime."

Trevor glanced at me and smiled. It was the first smile of his that I'd seen since the country club.

"But don't expect an invite to Christmas dinner at Richard's," Edward said and laughed.

"They are welcome at our house any time," said Vivian. "I'm glad someone finally put him in his place."

"I take it that they've asked Kennedy to join the practice?" Trevor asked.

"Yes, but I hardly think she's going to accept now. She stormed out right after the two of you left," James said, shaking his head. "Anyway, this night was supposed to be about you, and while we can't make it up to you, we would like to take you two to dinner to celebrate your job - and your engagement."

Vivian walked over to Trevor and gave him a peck on the cheek.

"You did a good job, Trevor," Vivian said.

"Not only with the ring, but with the one wearing it," Claire chimed in.

"So glad you approve," Trevor's sarcasm hadn't abated any.

He turned to look at me.

"Dinner?" he asked.

"This night is about you. I'm up for whatever you want to do."

"No, it's now about us," he said as he walked over to me, wrapping one arm around my waist.

I smiled.

"I'm up for anything, but I do need to do something first."

"Absolutely," he said and gave me a quick kiss before turning to his brothers and their wives. "As beautiful as you two ladies are, despite your questionable choices in men, I think I'd like to spend the rest of the evening with my fiancée."

I smiled.

"Wise choice," Edward said as he came behind Trevor and patted him on the shoulder. Trevor released me and headed to the door to show his brothers out.

"We want to do an engagement party," Vivian said. "I promise there won't be any exes invited."

"I'd like that. Thank you," I said as she gave me a huge hug.

"I'm so glad you're going to be part of our family," she said.

At the door, there were a series of obligatory hugs before they got into Edward's car and left.

"To your parents?" Trevor asked.

"Yes. I want them to hear it from me before the rest of Augusta tells them."

"Of course."

We visited my parents, and there were plenty of hugs and tears. Mama knew right away from the moment I entered the house. Daddy hugged me and whispered, "that one's a keeper, sweetheart," and he shook Trevor's hand.

After we spent some time with them, I got on a video chat with Emmie and Beth.

Lastly, I texted Zack to let him know Trevor had proposed.

16

As beautiful as the weekend was, Monday morning came sooner than I wanted. I was back in the shop, and Trevor was at the medical college. There wasn't much for me to do except prepare for the weekend. I needed to make sure I had enough flowers coming in to cover the upcoming weddings. Beth and Emmie wouldn't be in until later, so I had time to myself. I sipped on some cold, sweet tea while I checked the headlines from the paper and at the TV websites.

Debbie had been arrested and charged with the theft of more than $500,000. The stories said federal charges were pending in the money laundering case because it went beyond Georgia state lines. There was also a story that Becca had been arrested, but it wasn't a long one.

Both of those news items hurt. I breathed a conflicted sigh. Part of me was happy my work was done, but at the same time, my heart was heavy for Jimmy. I really cared about him, and it bothered me that I never realized how unhappy he was. I never knew what was hiding behind his smile. People always said I was the sensitive one, but I'd missed this. I'd probably kick myself for that for many years to come. I wanted it to be a regular Monday when Jimmy was in the doghouse and needed my assistance to bail him out. I wanted to tell him I was engaged to Trevor. But I knew that wouldn't come. I sat at my office computer and stared at the screen. I heard the bells jingle, and I walked out into my shop to see Drew. He was holding two white paper cups and a white bag. I eyed him suspiciously. He knew what had happened Saturday evening, and I was apprehensive as I placed my left hand behind my back.

"Good morning," he said. "I brought this for you."

My movement didn't go unnoticed. He shook his head "no" at me. His face fell. The five o'clock shadow and the dark circles under his eyes betrayed the fact that he hadn't slept in a while. He held out one of the paper cups to me. I hesitated.

"It's not poisoned," he snarked and took a sip of it to prove it to me. He handed me the other cup.

"Good morning, Drew. I'll take the one you drank out of," I took the cup and a new straw from him and slowly sipped in the cold, sweet tea. It was so good. "I wasn't expecting to see you this morning."

He smiled faintly at me. It was an odd smile – a forced one filled with sadness.

"You're glowing this morning," he said. His voice was hoarse. "I haven't seen you look like that in a long time."

I glanced at the floor.

"Thanks."

"I wanted to offer my congratulations," he said clearing his throat. "And I wanted to update you on the case."

"Thank you. I guess you talked to Zack; he didn't tell me."

He nodded slowly.

"Zack paid me a visit on Saturday night, plus I got phone calls from Emmie and Beth. They took great pleasure in calling me."

"I didn't put them up to that."

"I know you didn't. Zack stayed and babysat me to make sure I didn't relapse."

"I'm sorry."

"Stop saying that, Grace. There's nothing for you to be sorry about. You let me know where you stand. This is my fault. I'm the one who is sorry," he paused. "But things sure went quickly."

I couldn't stop the smile from crossing my lips.

"Thanks," I paused. "Let's talk about something else. You didn't have to bring me breakfast."

"It's a small token of my thanks. Besides, I'm starved. I needed to tell you something about the case, and I thought it would be rude to bring my breakfast without at least offering you some."

"What happened?" I motioned for Drew to follow me into my office.

We sat down across from each other as he handed me my sweet tea and a Morning Glory muffin. He had coffee and a breakfast sandwich.

"Well, some things didn't add up, and you felt it too. I told you how Jimmy was killed. It was a gunshot wound to the back of his head."

That still sent a chill down my spine. I moved uncomfortably in my chair.

"Yes, you did, Drew, so there was no way anyone struggled over a gun and accidently fired it. Someone stood directly behind him to kill him."

"That's correct. That's the first thing that didn't add up. But there was something else that didn't add up. There was only one set of fingerprints on the gun," he said.

I shook my head.

"I don't follow you, Drew."

"Well, we knew that Jimmy had decided to kill himself. It was in the letter he left you," he said.

"Yes."

"The murder weapon was registered to Jimmy. If he'd planned on using that and there was a struggle as she claimed, then Jimmy's prints would've been on there as well as Becca's."

I nodded slowly.

"I asked Becca about that, and she couldn't answer. I called Jake in, and it turns out that Becca was covering for him."

"She what?"

"Yeah. She was going to take the rap."

"I don't understand. She lied to protect Jake?" I was confused. I didn't think they were that close.

"Not to protect Jake. Apparently, Jake called his dad the night he died. While on the phone, he tried to talk him out of committing suicide. It worked. Jake got to his dad, and he was still alive."

"And?"

"Jake said he doesn't remember what happened after that. He just remembers arguing with Jimmy."

"What happened?"

"Details are sketchy. I have conflicting stories. Becca has tried to stand by her story, but it has more holes than a slice of Swiss cheese. Here's where it gets interesting. Jake said he went to talk Jimmy out of killing himself, and Jimmy let it slip that he'd cut Jake out of the will. Jimmy had cut him off financially. I think Jake was trying to get some money out of him. That lake property and the car was supposed to go to Jake not you. He and Jimmy worked on it together. Cal hasn't been completely honest either."

I swallowed and looked down. My heart was breaking for Jimmy.

"I wished I'd been more of the person he thought I was. I didn't think I'd done anything special just by listening to him."

"Grace, sometimes, that's all people have, and it probably didn't help that Jake was high on something, and in his rage, he killed Jimmy."

"Why did she confess? And why did you zone in on her at the cemetery if you knew it wasn't her?"

"Her body language told me she knew something. Jake kept it together surprisingly well."

"He was sweating up a storm, Drew. But then again we all were."

"Yeah, Grace. He was nervous. I didn't arrest her there. I just brought her in for questioning. And I asked her a few pointed questions. I really think she thought Clint killed Jimmy, and she was trying to protect the man she loves. I talked to Clint, who also had a disagreement with Jimmy on the night he died. Clint wanted to borrow some money to buy a new rig, but Jimmy didn't want to help him. And I checked Jimmy's phone records. She had talked to him about 15 minutes before Jake called him. He must've confessed to her what he planned to do, and she tried to talk him out of it."

"I knew that Jimmy didn't like Clint. Anytime I asked Jimmy how Becca was he talked about her 'no good' boyfriend, who was bad with money and loose with women. I think that's how he described him. He also called him a bum. He said he hadn't driven a truck in months and was mooching off Becca."

"Anyway, Clint said he went to ask one more time for a loan. Jimmy turned him down. He said that when he left, Jimmy was still alive."

"So, how did you find out it was Jake, Drew?"

"The T-shirt didn't have Clint's DNA on it, but it did have Jake's."

"Wow. What a waste. Nothing makes sense."

"None of it makes sense. Murder never makes any sense to me. It's all a waste, Grace," he said. "Oh, and thanks to the information Jimmy left us, Steve is probably going to be brought up on racketeering charges. He's a slick one. Jimmy borrowed money from him not knowing that Steve had his dealings with a lot of shady stuff. Steve wanted the money back with interest and other things. And with the information you gave me about Beth and the Ponzi scheme, the FBI will have even more ammunition. They had a lot of things they held over Jimmy's head. It was a messy situation. Jake may have been involved with them too. I don't know. It's a big mess."

"Drew, I have a couple of questions that I never got answered."

He tilted his head.

"Okay. What are they?"

"Well, how did the murder weapon and shirt get to the lake?"

"Clint called Becca after he left Jimmy's office. He was angry and told her he wanted to kill her dad. Peggy told Becca about the phone call from your mom and how worried you were. She went to check on Jimmy and found him dead. Sometime between Clint's visit and Becca going to the office, Jake confronted and killed Jimmy. Jake had stripped off the shirt and left it and the gun on the floor. I told you he was high. He wasn't in his right mind. Becca knew about the lake house. She even had a key. We can charge her for tampering with the crime scene. She removed the gun and shirt and took them to the lake house."

"Why didn't she throw the evidence into the lake? Or any number of places in the 30 minutes it took her to get there. I mean, she was right there. That made no sense."

"Do you have any idea how much that gun was worth?"

"No. I mean I knew that it was from Jimmy's collection and that Peggy was super angry when he bought it. But that's all I know."

Drew laughed.

"That particular antique handgun could've been worth a lot of money to a collector," Drew said. "It's super rare. It could've paid for a new rig for Clint and then some. For an item like that one, collectors can be hush-hush about where they got it. And she was hoping it would never get connected to Jimmy's murder."

"Wow. It was worth that much?"

Drew nodded slowly.

"Oh yeah. It was worth a lot. And that Camaro. It was worth a lot too," he paused. "Becca said she wasn't sure what to do about the shirt. She heard Cal who was coming back from night fishing. She got spooked because she heard him shaking the doorknob on the side of the building. She didn't want him to find her in the garage. She hid, and then when the coast was clear, she headed out. She'd planned to come back later for the shirt because by then Peggy was calling her wanting to know where she was. And who was going to be looking for that? She had no idea that Jimmy would tell anyone about that place."

"Another question was about the meeting that Peggy said Jimmy had to get the money to cover Jake's debts."

Drew shook his head.

"I checked his financials and his calendar. The only meetings Jimmy had had during the past few months were with his lawyers. He made sure that those kids and Peggy couldn't touch his assets."

My head started pounding as I tried to process everything.

"I think his meeting was with a bottle and a gun," he said.

"I never asked you if he had been drinking."

Drew nodded slowly.

"Alcohol numbs the pain, and he knew he could do what he intended if he was drunk."

"I hate all this, Drew."

"I know."

I shook my head slowly, trying not to cry again.

"Jimmy kept saying he'd made a lot of mistakes he was sorry for."

"I can't answer that. He didn't do anything illegal. He just made bad choices, and alienating his kids and wife were probably the result of some of those bad choices he made."

I glanced at him.

"Was Peggy having an affair?"

"No, Grace. Steve Mathis just wanted money, but he's a smooth talker. He played on her emotions; he made her feel like a young woman again. He was using her the whole time," he said. "She broke down when I gave her that ring box and note Jimmy left for her."

"I can't imagine," I said. "My heart hurts thinking about all of it."

He looked at me and smiled.

"You're six for six," Drew said.

"What are you talking about?"

"You. You've helped me solve all six cases we've worked on together."

I nodded. It was a hollow victory if you could even call it a victory.

"You know, Grace, we're both wrong about something."

"What's that?"

"I told you we didn't work, and you told me I was right."

"Drew, it's true."

"Not completely," he said softly. "When I finally started listening to you about your dreams, you helped me solve cases. And I think we make a good team. Thank you."

I didn't answer.

"And I also want to thank you again for showing me what unconditional love looks like," he said. "I think most women would've wanted to get revenge, and if it had been anyone else, they would've let me rot in jail at Christmas. People might say you're weak, but to love someone and believe in someone who has betrayed and hurt you, takes a lot of inner strength and character. You definitely have that, and I know where it comes from. Grace is the perfect name for you because you gave me more grace than I ever deserved."

I could feel tears welling in my eyes. I took a deep breath.

"You need to stop because I don't want to start blubbering. You're making me sound like a saint."

He smiled.

"Grace, I know you aren't that. I lived with you for more than 10 years," he said, pausing briefly. "And I wish you and Trevor the greatest happiness. That's all I've ever wanted for you. I'm just sorry I wasn't the one who could make you happy."

"Drew, you and I had a lot of good years. It was only in the past two or three that things got difficult."

He laughed.

"Difficult? Is that all you'd call them?"

"Yeah. I think so. I think I'm a better person for my time with you though. Thank you for breakfast."

He stood up to leave.

"Now what are you working on?" I asked as I followed him to the door.

He turned and smiled.

"Since we're such a good team, do you want to help me on it?" he laughed.

"No, I'm good I think."

"Hmm, I remember you telling me about a year ago that you might be up for detective work."

"That was a year ago, and hey, I've got a perfect record, so I think I should quit while I'm ahead."

He smiled at me.

"Glad to hear it, Grace."

He headed to the door, but he paused right before opening it. He turned and leaned over to kiss me on my forehead.

"Be happy, Grace. Trevor is a good man, and I know he loves you."

I could feel the tears welling in my eyes. I touched his cheek.

"Take care of yourself, detective."

He nodded and left the building. The glass door closed behind him, and I watched him head to his car. I touched the door's metal frame, and as I did, I saw the ring on my left hand. I smiled. Maybe all things did work out for the good.

Other books by Charmain Zimmerman Brackett

Grace's Augusta Mysteries
Murder Under the Magnolias
Murder En Pointe
Murder Makes the Ballot
Murder Makes a Mistake
Murder Takes a Bow

Victoria James Mystery Series
Paperback
Murder Run Deep (Book 1)
Murder's Deep Secret (Book 2)

Key Guardian Journal series
The Key of Elyon
Elyon's Cipher
Elyon's Light: Lucy's Call

Fixed in the Tempest

Children's titles
Little Pearl's Circus World
Nutcrackers and Pirates: A Boy's Journey Into Dance

Contact the author at czbblog@gmail.com.

Find her on Facebook at www.facebook.com/thekeyofelyon or on Twitter @CZBrackett